PROPERTY OF
PROWLER

book 1

KINGS OF ANARCHY MC

NEVADA

I0642707

VERLENE LANDON

COPYRIGHT

This author does NOT host her stories on any pay-per-chapter (PPC) apps or websites.

If you find this (or other books by Verlene Landon) on those apps/sites, they are there illegally.

Trusted source links can be found on my website.

Any similarities to real persons, organizations, or places written about within these pages is purely coincidental, as this is a work of fiction.

Editing/Proof: My Brother's Editor
Editing/Proof: Romance Revisions
Cover Design: GChelle Designs
Cover Photographer: CJC Photography/Christopher John
Cover Models: Kim & Bri

ISBN: 979-8-9867605-9-9

Kings of Anarchy MC Code

Anarchy - Where the Kings rule in chaos

Respect the Mother Chapter
Your **loyalty** stays with your patch
Brotherhood above all
Never touch another brother's ol' lady
Ride or **die**, no questions asked
Never back down from a **fight**
Never let a **brother** ride solo
Each chapter sets its own **damn** rules

<u>Motto</u>

Nobody fucks with the Kings

www.kingsofanarchymc.com

KOAMC NEVADA

Book One

President - Prowler
Vice President - Bulldog
SGT at Arms/Enforcer - Ghoul
Road Captain - Monster
Secretary - Kansas
Treasurer - Boogeyman
Tail Gunner - Chef

Members
Creedence, Golden
Incarcerated Members
Hunter, Sleeper

Family
Cassidy (Prowler's daughter)

JUST SO YOU KNOW

This book contains adult themes, situations, and language.

There may also be scenes which some readers might find disturbing.

If you need or desire more in-depth information to make an informed choice of what you read, visit https://verlenelandon.com/propertyofprowler/

A King in dusty leather is better than a knight in shining armor.

PROWLER

As president of the Nevada chapter of the Kings of Anarchy MC, Prowler has his fair share of secrets. To protect his club and their secrets, he keeps everyone who isn't family at arm's length.

He opts for a no-strings situationship with his sexy neighbor, but things start to get very stringy after he realizes she's his mate.

TAYLOR

When her abusive ex got arrested for the third time, Taylor knew she had to run. She changed her appearance, her name, and even worked as a legal escort to carve out a new life for herself.

A life that she thinks is perfect. That is until she breaks the biggest rule of the neighbors-with-benefits arrangement she has with Prowler ... she falls in love.

When Taylor runs, Prowler pursues, but can his wolf catch her before her past does?

To the super nice guy at the Nekrogoblikon concert in Las Vegas on June 8, 2025, who threw my cup away for me so I didn't lose my place close to the rail, thank you so much. You rock!

PROWLER

"Sitting on your front porch, nursing a cold one with your eyes set on ..." Ghoul scanned around and clicked his tongue. "On the neighbor's place. Interesting." Being extra observant wasn't a bad quality in an SAA—or a mountain lion—but he damn sure hated it when someone turned those skills on him.

Prowler's private life wasn't for his club's consumption unless he was taking an ol' lady, and that wasn't on the table and never would be.

"Fuck you."

As far as quips went, it wasn't eloquent, but it got the job done.

"You don't wanna fuck *me*, Prez, I think you

wanna fuck that sexy-ass stripper across the way
... *again*."

"She's not a stripper," Prowler snarled at the
same time Bulldog spoke.

"Prez is smarter than to shit where he eats.
Besides, Cassidy would tear him a new one."

The look his vice gave him said he knew
Prowler had slept with her already, he just didn't
approve. The burly bear of a vice president
brought up his daughter just to judge his reaction.
He knew it.

Wait, what did Ghoul say again?

How many times did his SAA know about, he
wondered.

Monster pinged his gaze back and forth
between Prowler and Bulldog, landing on his Prez.

"Casino floor dancer is just a family-friendly
version of a stripper." His tone was just matter-of-
fact, not arrogant or judgmental.

Then Monster turned his gaze to his vice.

"Amen. Getting involved with someone who
can see your house from their living room is a fast
track to slashed tires, boiled bunnies, and a knife
in the back as soon as you fall dick first into your
next snatch."

Fuck, he knew it too. Trying to keep a secret from a bunch of shifters was impossible.

Monster looked to Chef, the only non-shifter, but he just threw up his hands.

"I have no opinion on Prez's personal life." Chef replied.

Good man.

Not getting the response he wanted from Chef, their road captain swigged his beer.

He wasn't wrong. Especially since Taylor was the one who watched his daughter when he had her, but club business or shifts kept him busy.

His brothers may know he was sleeping with her now, but did they know it had been going on for months?

He and Taylor had a regular arrangement, and thank God Cassidy was none the wiser.

When they needed an itch scratched, they scratched it. Then, depending on which bed they fell into, one of them went back to their own home as soon as the deed was done. No muss, no fuss, and most importantly, no strings.

They were on the same page about that and thank fuck, because he enjoyed her body while neither caught feelings other than bliss. That didn't come along every day, so he was loath to lose it.

It was just sex, and it was convenient. They'd agreed when it no longer was, they'd stop fucking but nothing else would change. Especially since she watched Cassidy for him.

Prowler wasn't keen on getting his dick wet with any of the girls who worked at their brothel. Community property wasn't his thing and never would be. To say he'd never let more than one of them blow him would be a lie though.

Nor did he want to put in the effort to date anyone. Sitting around a steakhouse while making small talk just for a slim chance to get his rocks off wasn't for him either.

Nope, a relationship with as many secrets as he had would never work, nor did he want that.

The current arrangement with Taylor worked just fine, perfect in fact.

"That ship already sailed," Kansas declared.

Prowler snapped his gaze to his secretary. Not that he'd explicitly told him to keep his mouth shut. He'd assumed it was implied.

Kansas was the only one who'd been raised in a pack, so all shifter questions went directly to him.

So, apparently more of his club knew he was fucking his neighbor than he'd realized.

"Aw, fuck," a few of his brothers cursed.

"You getting jailed by some pussy, Prez?"

"Hell no. Been there, done that, got the court documents to prove it."

His ex was relentless. Prowler didn't have any issues with child support. Hell, he wanted his daughter to have everything and loved her beyond reason. All the shit with Allie was worth it because Cassidy existed.

It was the alimony that pissed him off.

It was Allie constantly using their daughter to try to get him back and pulling shit that didn't serve anyone but herself.

It was the smiling and nodding while keeping his mouth shut for his daughter's sake that felt like it was crushing his soul.

"Famous last words," Ghoul declared with finality.

"Bullshit. My ex is enough to remind me not to make that mistake again."

Prowler didn't do feelings anymore, nor did he plan to start. He'd done that once, and it damn near did him in when he caught Allie with another man in their own bed while his daughter slept in the next room.

That was the first time he'd ever killed a man.

It was also how he found himself sharing his body with a wolf.

While he'd love to say it had been a crime committed in the heat of passion killing, it wasn't. He'd calmly told Allie to get dressed, take his daughter, get a hotel room, and not to return until the next day, all while holding a gun to the naked man's head.

The voices of the past pelted him.

"Riley, what are you going to do? Riley, don't hurt him. Riley this, Riley that."

He'd tuned her out until he heard the door close behind her. That soft snick was like a starter pistol.

Instantly, he'd dropped the gun and beaten the man to death with his bare hands. Apparently, the moment the asshole had tried to shift was when he'd drawn his last breath. All with Prowler's hands wailing on him.

Prowler learned the hard way that a wolf can transfer.

Every fucking movie had so much wrong about shifters. From what they could and couldn't scent in human form to ways to kill them. It wasn't a bite that made wolves. It could happen at the moment of death. And the scent thing was exaggerated by Hollywood, at least for those who came into their wolf by accident.

By the time Allie had returned the next day with Cassidy, all the evidence of his crime was gone, and his life was forever changed.

The day after that, he'd filed for divorce.

He'd never told Allie what had happened, though she'd asked hundreds of times over the years.

It didn't really matter if she knew or not; he'd agreed to a ridiculous amount of alimony and all her other terms in the divorce to get rid of her.

The only thing he'd contested was more time with his daughter. Another zero added to Allie's monthly payment got him that.

"Speak of the devil, and she shall appear." Ghoul's words pulled him from the past. Following his gaze, there was Allie, pulling up his drive in a brand-new sports car.

Prowler'd bought her a perfectly adequate and safe *mom* car for his daughter's sake just a few years ago. It pissed him off to no end that she wasn't driving it.

When Cassidy emerged from the passenger side, all thoughts of Allie and the past fled. He couldn't stop the joy that crossed his face. The smile she gifted him was a mirror of his own before she turned to wave across the street.

Taylor was putting out her garbage cans. How had he not noticed?

Her dark hair was piled on her head messily, and the half-shirt and cut-off short combo made his mouth water. Parts of tattoos and curves on full display. The memory of tracing the hidden ink with his tongue didn't help suppress the wave of desire that flared to life at seeing her.

Not that he didn't appreciate her all made up because he damn sure loved that vampy shit. When she was headed to work, she put on a ton of makeup and a sparkly costume that hardened his dick, but the more toned-down version was hot too. Just in a different way.

"Hey, Sassy Cassy," Taylor greeted his daughter. "Wanna watch *Tombstone* and gorge on vegan pizza later?" she shouted across the way.

Prowler had already asked Taylor to hang out with his daughter as he had a long-standing appointment to keep followed by a run.

Vegas was too densely developed for a half

pack of wolves, and a few other assorted animals, to be running around the city. The area around the prison was perfect. Acres and acres of unpopulated desert landscape.

So, without fail, every week, a handful of brothers went for a run after visiting Hunter and Sleeper. That way their club brothers were taken care of, and the free brothers got to sprout fur for a few hours.

Hunter was a natural, and the guilt over having to suppress his brother's wolf never left him. While Prowler and his wolf had yet to bond, he still couldn't imagine suppressing that presence entirely.

"I'm your huckleberry," his daughter yelled back across the street in a fake accent, before turning to him.

Setting his beer down, Prowler stood and opened his arms. Cass flew into them. Her head was at shoulder level, and he was six-one. Yeah, she took after her dad.

"How much did you grow in two weeks, Jellybean? I didn't authorize that."

Cassidy groaned, probably rolling her eyes. "Dad, I love you, but you have got to get a new line already."

"No way, kiddo. I think the one I got is perfectly fine." It was the same exchange every time, and it was comforting. He'd take it as long as he could get it. Before long, his daughter would be into all the things that drew teenage girls away from their dads. No way was he giving that up without a fight.

"Why do you let that hooker watch *my* daughter?" Leave it to Allie to spoil the moment by spewing venom. It wasn't surprising. It's what she did. She lived for the drama.

Before he could correct his ex, yet again, his daughter turned out of his embrace to face her mother.

"Taylor's not a hooker, and I am more than just *your* daughter. I have a name."

Prowler kissed the top of her head. "Go on inside, Jellybean. I got you a surprise. It's in your room. Take your time. I've gotta talk to your mother for a few."

Without protest, she followed his command. Once his daughter was inside, he turned to Allie.

Prowler stepped off the porch and toward his ex. "Cut your shit in front of Cassidy, Allie. And what's with that?" He pointed toward the car, then crossed his arms over his chest, widening his stance.

"I'm obviously paying you too much alimony if you can splurge like that. Where's the car I bought?" He didn't add *on top of what I already pay you,* but it was on the tip of his tongue.

Anger raced across her face, and her eyes narrowed before she changed tactics, her tone turning sickeningly sweet. At one time he found it kind of sexy, now it made him cringe.

"Oh, I didn't spend a dime on that beauty. It was a gift."

"Who's calling who a hooker?"

The question was barely audible, but Prowler recognized Ghoul's dry delivery, even at a whisper. So did Allie, because she snapped her head around so fast, it was a wonder she didn't give herself whiplash.

"I'm nothing like that bitch. My man buys me nice things because he loves me. She's just a piece of ass."

Did everyone know he was sleeping with Taylor? Was it the worst kept secret in Vegas or what?

Monster was the one to defend Taylor, and it irritated Prowler slightly.

"She bought her own car, so—"

Prowler interrupted with the most important point with a voice that was too hopeful.

"When's the wedding?" The sooner the bitch got married, the sooner he could stop paying her blood money.

Allie looked over her shoulder before stepping into his body, turning her face back to kiss him on the mouth. He was so shocked he didn't pull away first, and something told him that would come back to haunt him later. Instead, her words, spoken practically against his lips, were the icing on a shit sundae.

"Oh, lover, that'll never happen. No matter who we fuck, we'll always belong to each other." Her voice was a purr as her hand trailed down his chest before she spun on her heels and strutted back to her car.

All he could do was watch her walk away with his jaw slack. He'd never be free of that harpy, even with Hunter and Sleeper's sacrifice.

Right before she opened her door, she blew a kiss and waved across the street. He looked up to see Taylor still standing there, hands on her garbage can and frozen in place, kinda like him.

Only she looked hurt while he was simply defeated.

"Fuck," he growled.

He and Taylor had nothing more between them than sex. Convenient, no-strings-attached sex. The only caveat they'd agreed upon was that when they decided to scratch that itch elsewhere, they'd end their arrangement and go back to normal.

They'd still be neighbors, and she'd still watch Cass, but there would be no animosity because it wasn't a relationship. That didn't mean he wanted to hurt her.

Thanks to his enhanced vision, even when he had not shifted, he could see the pain in her peridot eyes. Even if he couldn't see her eyes, her posture and body language gave it away.

Exactly as Allie had intended.

Bitch.

He raised his hand to beckon her over, but she just crossed her arms.

Fuck, he didn't want to try to clear this up by shouting across the street, especially in front of half of his club. They were already giving him shit. He didn't need to give them more fuel for the fire, but fuck if he could leave it as a misunderstanding.

As much as he told himself it was just sex, he did have some fond feelings toward Taylor. Who wouldn't?

"Come over a few minutes early?" he yelled across the street.

"No can do." She spoke a little too casually, but the undertone said it all. Her voice was unsteady. Why did he feel so twisted up over it? They were casual. It was the beauty of their arrangement. But her pain irritated him and his wolf. Which made zero fucking sense because he and his wolf weren't as meshed as those who were born to it were.

His wolf didn't even choose him. He was just the only vessel there when his previous companion died. Their relationship was different. They didn't blend. Instead, they came to a tense but acceptable cohabitation situation. His wolf didn't speak to him the way natural wolves did. They merely existed in the same body. So, yeah, no mate-drive like in the books.

"I've already ordered the pizza and queued up the movie. Send Cass over whenever she's ready."

The smile and wave that followed were too

fake for his liking. Watching her turn and walk toward her door twisted a knife in his gut.

They had a good thing, and he hated that Allie could fuck that up for him. He was so over her and her bullshit. Thirteen goddamn years was too fucking long for her to still be fucking his life to hell and back.

Raking his hand through his hair for what felt like the millionth time, he cursed again.

"Fuck."

Prowler was seconds away from marching across the street and setting Taylor's fine ass straight. She was his for now. Only his daughter's voice from behind stopped him.

"Thanks, Dad. I love it." She wrapped her arms around him from behind. She had the portable pink gaming system he'd gotten her in one hand, while a backpack hung from her other shoulder.

"You bet, Jellybean. Anything you want—it's yours, you know that."

"Maybe this weekend we can cook dinner together?" Of course he would agree, but before he could, she added, "And invite Taylor?" He knew a setup when he smelled one, but again, he was powerless when it came to his daughter.

He also liked the idea. Maybe he could smooth

things over, and Taylor could stay after Cass went to bed. The more he thought about it, the more he liked it. Taylor was mush for his daughter, and he was not above exploiting that.

"Sure, kiddo." The smile she gifted him was life.

"I can't wait to tell her. See ya." She bounded down the drive and across the street.

"I've got fifty that says Prez takes an ol' lady within the week," one of his brothers says. He would be hard-pressed to say who because he was laser-focused on his daughter.

"I'll take that action," another answered. He didn't divert his attention until his daughter let herself into Taylor's place.

Once she was safe, he turned to his brothers at large.

"Ready?"

"Let's ride." His brothers voiced their agreement.

Before the four of them left, he turned to Chef and Boogeyman. "Watch my girls."

Ghoul had the biggest shit-eating grin on his face before he donned his helmet.

It wasn't lost on Prowler that he'd said *my*

girls, but it felt right, at least at that particular moment.

"I'll guard what's *yours* as if it were mine." Boogey smirked.

That should've irritated him, but it didn't. He really didn't want to do a relationship ever again, but his wolf seemed to sit up on his haunches at the idea.

Somehow his casual fuck was headed that direction, and he felt powerless to stop it.

As long as he didn't let on to Taylor that he might be catching feelings, their arrangement didn't need to change.

2

TAYLOR

"What the hell was I thinking?" Taylor asked the dishes she was banging into the dishwasher.

"I knew better than that. I knew. Too damn sexy. But hey, I always gotta fall for the bad boys, huh?"

She slammed her favorite coffee mug a little too hard and broke it.

"Fuck," she cursed as she sucked the blood off her finger.

"No, no, no, no," she cried and fished out pieces of her CUNT mug.

Cursing herself some more, she tossed them in the trash and finished cleaning up the kitchen.

Taylor had zero intentions of sleeping with her

sexy-ass biker neighbor when he'd moved in. That lasted all of about six months.

Then, when they did come to an arrangement, she resolved not to fall for him. Just sex, which is all either of them wanted.

What is it they say about best-laid plans? Yeah, that. It only took about two months of a steady diet of his cock and tongue, and her traitorous cunt was falling and taking Taylor down with her.

She wasn't head over heels in love, but she definitely had some fonder than *like* feelings for her tall, blond Viking of a biker neighbor. That thought came with a metric fuckton of complications.

They had an agreement, and "fonder than like" was strictly forbidden.

Cassidy.

Fuck, if she told Prowler how she was starting to fall when she promised not to catch feels, he'd definitely distance himself and his daughter. She'd miss Cass so much if that happened.

They'd promised each other when they were done being neighbors-with-benefits, things would go back to normal. They'd remain neighborly, and she'd still watch Cass.

However, they never discussed what would happen if one of them fell for the other. Frankly, they were both one hundred and ten percent convinced it would never happen.

Taylor for damn sure never expected it. Hell, the first time she'd even realized it herself was just minutes ago. When his ex was all over him, and he did fuck all to stop it.

She felt like a moron just standing there stupefied while it happened. She'd wanted nothing more than to either rip Allie's hair out or to turn and go back inside, but she didn't do either ... couldn't.

When Allie had kissed him, though, Taylor felt like she couldn't breathe. That's when it'd hit her. She caught feelings.

The scene stung hard, and not just because she'd kinda, maybe, sorta, fallen, but that Prowler would've allowed it. With everywhere their tongues had been when they were together at night, they didn't kiss, not really. He'd go to town between her legs, and she'd swallow his load, but they didn't kiss on the lips.

So, in witnessing that, it had been a moment of truth for Taylor. Not just with the realization she had fallen for him, but that there was still something between Prowler and Allie. Something she couldn't, and wouldn't, compete with. Granted, she'd broken their rule by falling, but he didn't know that. Kissing his ex on the mouth was devastating to Taylor.

With that in mind, she had no intention of ever, ever telling Prowler how she felt or that she was fostering those feelings. No, she would shove them down until they dissipated.

She couldn't keep sleeping with him, though. Not now that her heart had entered the chat. Being intimate with him would just nurture any feelings she harbored. But boy, would she miss that. Prowler was an exceptional lover and a good man.

Her ex was the exact opposite of Prowler in that aspect. Still a bad boy, but of the loser flavor. It had taken her a year of working a job she wasn't proud of to dig out of the financial hole he'd left her in.

Once she had, she moved to Vegas, changed everything, even her name, and had been self-reliant ever since. And, just last year, she'd finally stopped looking over her shoulder waiting for Billy to find her like he'd promised. He said he'd kill her if she ever left him, and she'd believed it.

That's why she took the job as a legal escort while he was locked up for one of his short stints.

Billy never thought to look for her that close to home or as an escort of all things. Hell, they'd had top-class security there, so it had been perfect.

She knew Billy had half-heartedly looked when he'd first got out, and that's when she high-tailed it to Vegas and changed her name, her hair —everything she could do to change her appearance at first glance.

The best part was her nose. The third and final time he'd broken it, she'd had to have surgery, but he'd gotten pinched before the bandages came off. He had no idea how different her face looked, all thanks to him.

Kind of poetic to her way of thinking. It was his constant abuse that made it hard for her to be recognized by him or any of his loser buddies, even when she'd come face-to-face with one of them.

Tommy, Billy's childhood friend, had tried to tip her a fifty-dollar chip to come down and "be his good luck charm," and he was none the wiser to who she was.

She'd almost shit a gold brick. Scared her so

bad, she faked the flu, took a week off, and didn't leave the house.

Nightmares still plagued her occasionally, but she'd heard Billy lost interest when he replaced her with a new woman willing to put up with his selfish lovemaking and financial dependency.

But when she'd seen his face on the news, going down for another nickel, that's when she truly could breathe and started living.

"I am swearing off bad boys, all flavors. Maybe I'll find a nice accountant type who plays pickle-ball or something."

She poured herself a huge soda. "Yep. That's the plan. Move on from old habits," she pep-talked herself aloud while waiting for the foam to dissipate so she could top off her drink.

Having a plan made her feel a little better, even if her grand plan consisted of telling Prowler she was ending their happy, happy fun time, per their prior agreed-upon conditions. That way, things could go back to normal, and she would still get to have Cass in her life.

Taylor didn't want kids, never did, and never would, but Cass was something different. She wasn't just the child of the man Taylor was having sex with. She didn't see Cass in that way.

Cassidy was more like a friend, as weird as it sounded, if it were socially acceptable for a grown-ass woman to hang out with a fourteen-year-old.

With a new resolve to end her addiction to the wrong men once and for all, she headed to the living room.

The beeping on her front door told her someone was entering the code. Within seconds, Cass called out.

"Taylor, look what my dad got me." She came bounding into the living room with a handheld gaming system, handing it to Taylor as she plopped on the couch next to her.

"Oh, this is *noice*." Taylor spoke in an over-the-top voice before handing it back.

Prowler was an amazing father. Seeing him with Cassidy had been the thing that tipped her over the *should I sleep with him* line.

While she didn't have that biological drive to have kids, a man doing dad stuff and loving it was still sexy as fuck.

Prowler had predator written all over him, but when he looked at his daughter, every fiber of the man's body changed. She couldn't help but finally say yes when he extended the invitation to his bed yet again. That had been months ago, and they hadn't stopped banging like bunnies since.

But that was done. Hotel Vajayjay was closed. No vacancy.

"Earth to Taylor." Cassidy's voice broke through her internal ranting.

"Shit." She got up and followed Cass to the door where the guy stood smiling a little too flirtatiously as he handed over the white box.

Taylor gave him the stink eye as he leered at Cass walking away from him with their dinner. The way he pursed his lips while leaning sideways and watching her ass was gross. "She's a kid, you jackass." She slammed the door in his face.

"That perv will not be delivering here again," Taylor declared with finality.

"Write your bad review, or whatever people your age do, but just don't tell Dad, okay? He'll do something all *overprotective dad*-like."

Cass opened the box and served them both a slice, handing Taylor her plate, then proceeding to the couch.

Taylor followed. She mirrored Cass as she sat. One leg tucked under her backside, the other toeing the carpet, half facing each other and half facing the TV at the same time.

"First off, drop the *people my age* crap. I'm not ancient." She knew Cass was teasing; she always did. "Second, your dad is levelheaded."

Cass just stared in disbelief, and it was all Taylor could do not to laugh.

It wasn't an out-and-out lie.

Taylor had never witnessed him in a hot-headed moment, but there wasn't a doubt in her mind he had it in him lurking just under the surface, waiting to pounce if need be.

She took a bite of pizza, and that heavenly flavor exploded on her tongue ... kinda. Vegan pizza didn't exactly hit the same way. However, Cass had convinced her she could in fact live without cheese, but baby calves couldn't live without their mothers.

That and all the other gross things Cass had showed her about the dairy industry had her saying no thank you. That didn't mean she didn't miss the high that came from the first bite of ooey-gooey cheese, but she agreed it wasn't worth it. Pizza was still the perfect movie-watching entrée, vegan or not.

"Overprotective dad is what he's supposed to be. Chin up, kiddo. That's a good thing. Mine didn't protect me from squat." Least of all himself, she didn't add.

Cass brought her slice to her mouth, almost like she was hiding behind it. "Yeah, but his overprotective dad is leveled up."

Taylor just watched Cass take a bite and thoughtfully chew. Yeah, Prowler was in an MC, so there was no doubt they hurt people, but not just for fun.

That thought plagued her, though. Did Cass think he'd hurt someone willy-nilly?

If Taylor ignored Cass's concern, she would be no better that her own mom, who looked the other way when her husband had boundary issues with her only daughter or fast fists with his sons. If only someone had taken their off-handed comments seriously and asked the tough questions.

While she didn't get that vibe from Prowler, she wouldn't blow off Cass's concerns.

"Surely you don't mean ..." She didn't finish her question as Cass met her gaze. Taylor's heart cracked a little at the look in her blue eyes, identical to her father's blue eyes, except laced with uncertainty.

Surely, she didn't ... "Your dad would never

hurt *you*, Cass. I may not have had stellar examples of a good parent, but I don't think—" She caught herself defending him instead of listening to Cass. Again, that was her mother speaking from her mouth.

"Oh, god, no. I didn't mean that." Cass interrupted, horrified.

Thank God.

"I'm not saying my dad would hurt someone who cut him off in traffic or forgot the fire sauce with his tacos. I mean, guys like that." She nodded at the front door, where the pervy pizza man had ogled her. "He wouldn't hesitate if someone crosses anyone he considers family."

Taylor released the breath she'd been holding, bracing herself for ... she wasn't sure what.

She had to agree with Cass. Prowler would rip the guy apart if he knew how he'd looked at his daughter with the intentions that were clear in his gaze. Hell, any of his brothers would—it was just the way of life for them.

"It's one thing if he hurts real bad guys; it's another if he goes after a pizza guy who is just an idiot and looks barely out of high school. I don't want him to go to jail like Uncle Hunter and Uncle Sleeper. I may never see them again."

Cass's heartbreak was clear in her voice. Taylor knew about her incarcerated uncles. It was when she got to spend the most time with Cass. Prowler would get back late from his visits and sleep in the next day.

That had always made her curious. His prison visits shouldn't have been the most exhausting day of the man's week, but they always were.

While Prowler told her he visited them, he was vague about why it took so long. She had a sense that there was a lot more to it than taking too much time. She wasn't sure what, but the man had his secrets.

He carried a sawed-off wooden bat in his saddlebag, for fuck's sake. Plus, there was one just like it beside the front door, and a full-sized one under his bed. Either he was a closet baseball player for an underground midnight league for people who used short bats, or he was always expecting trouble.

In her experience, men who expected trouble that much usually did something to attract it.

Duh, he's an MC president.

She shook off those thoughts. This was about Cass, not her own fucked-up past that had her viewing everyone through blood-colored glasses.

"Lay it on me, sister. Tell me all your deepest, darkest secrets and fears, and I'll just listen. I pinky promise not to try to change the way you see it, laugh at you, or try to fix it if you don't want me to. What you feel is valid. Period, full stop."

Isn't that what every woman, regardless of age, wanted to hear?

With a sigh, Cass set her plate with a half-eaten piece of crust aside.

"You're so going to break one of those promises."

"Nope, I won't. Have I ever done you dirty?"

"No, you haven't, but it's so bizarre, even I don't believe it. I mean, I do, but I don't at the same time. I mean, shit, I probably shouldn't say anything." Cass had stood up and paced back and forth, chewing her lip. It was an action Taylor recognized. She was seriously questioning herself, and that sucked.

"Sweetie." Taylor reached up and grabbed her hand, stopping her back and forth, and pulled her back down to the sofa. "Spill. You obviously need to say it because it's eating away at you."

"So, first off, I know what being an MC president means. I'm not an idiot. I know Dad and my uncles have done things that are well ..." She trailed off. "But this is next level."

"Okay." What was bothering her more than what she already apparently knew about?

With a deep breath, Cass just blurts it out. "My dad's a shifter, a wolf to be exact," she said in a rush.

They just sat there for God only knew how long. The hamster had fallen off the wheel, and her brain went silent. Finally, the little fucker jumped back on the wheel but was sluggish as hell.

"What now?"

"My dad is a Jacob. At least I think he is. Like ninety-nine-point nine percent sure."

What could she say to that? Taylor thought she had at least a canned response to damn near anything to buy her time for a more thoughtful one, but this? Nope, she didn't have fuck all ready to go for *my dad sprouts fur*.

Surely Cass was using a metaphor or analogy or a simile or whatever the fuck you call it when something is like another thing, so you say it is. Taylor was a blackjack dealer and dancer, not a fucking English major.

"Why do you think he's like a wolf?"

"Not *like* a wolf, is a wolf. Alexander told me that shifters really exist, and then things started add—"

"Who's Alexander?"

"He's kinda my friend," Cass said shyly. "We have advanced math together. One day he told me that his brother's a shifter. He was in a car accident with his friend. His friend died, and that's how he became one. He was telling me things about his brother, like how he acts and stuff. It got me to thinking, so I started snooping. I think not only is Dad a wolf, but so is Uncle Hunter, and I think Uncle Monster and Uncle Golden are too. Maybe all of them. Well, no, not all. Uncle Sleeper isn't, and Uncle Bulldog is something else, but I don't know what."

Taylor just let her go until she couldn't take it anymore. Still chanting in her head, *don't invalidate and don't fix*, but what the fuck was she supposed to do? Cass must be going through something to be laying all this out there. She clearly believed it by how freaked out she was, and that is what scared Taylor the most. She may have to break confidence with Cass and tell Prowler for Cass's sake. It was the last thing she wanted to do.

"You don't think this Alexander kid is just making shit up because he wants to impress you?"

Cass's blush told her she was right, at least about Alexander liking her. "He does like me, and I like him, but that's not it. Alexander isn't supposed to say anything. He was really upset with himself when he did and begged me not to tell anyone."

Okay, so she wasn't going to get anywhere discrediting Alexander.

"Let's put a pin in the fact you didn't tell me you had a crush, which, ouch, by the way." Taylor wanted to focus on Alexander and Cass's first real crush, but she couldn't.

"Why do you think your dad is a shifter? Because he shares some traits with Alexander's brother who is supposedly a shifter?"

Taylor couldn't believe she was having a conversation about shifters. She considered herself very open-minded. She believed there was life on other planets, so why were shifters her sticking point?

Maybe because it makes a little too much sense.

Cass's eyes held a little bit of defeat, and Taylor's heart broke for her.

"I don't just think that, Tay. I'm telling you, *he*

is. You don't believe me?" Cass not only sounded hurt, but she also sounded disappointed in Taylor. "I thought you, of all people, would believe me."

"Sweetheart." Taylor grabbed both of her hands in her own.

"It's not that I don't believe *you*. But in order to do that, I have to change the way I have always looked at the world on a fundamental level."

Deep breath in and out.

"So, it's not you at all. It's reworking my idea of normal, and that takes time. Not because I don't believe you or don't want to, but shifters are something that only existed in movies and books my whole life, so give me some more information and let's see where that leads us. It could be that either one of us is mistaken."

There.

Taylor was rather proud of herself for that off-the-cuff, but diplomatic, response. She never wanted to hear that disappointment from Cass ever again.

"Okay, but get ready to have your mind blown." Cass pulled out a notebook.

Oh shit, little chick brought notes. Taylor was no psychologist, but was she inventing a fantasy world because of a shitty mom? Was it because she needed her dad to be a big bad shifter who would come in and eat the bad guys?

It wasn't like her dad wouldn't come in and decimate anyone who hurt his little girl already. Hell, that whole club would scorch the earth for her.

Cass had told her last month that her mom was seeing a new man, and she hated him. Maybe that's why she dove headfirst into Alexander's fantasy.

Taylor listened as Cass went through every single point she had. From why her dad was tired after the prison visits ... because that was when they shifted and ran in the unpopulated area around it... to eavesdropping on how they used a tattooed rune infused with silver to bind Hunter's wolf in prison so he wouldn't accidentally shift behind bars.

Taylor had to admit, if Cass's presentation was the opening scene of a movie, it was a pretty damn good one. Some of her points, Taylor herself had mused about. Cass's explanations fit so well, Taylor didn't have a clue how to explain it away from shifters into something more plausible.

Especially if she had actually overheard some of the things she thought she had. There's not a whole lot of wiggle room in binding a wolf with a tattooed silver rune.

Taylor shook her head. There had to be other explanations, like a weird Harley-worshiping cult or some shit. A secret society that emulated shifters.

Something.

"So, if your dad and some of your uncles are wolves, and Bulldog is a ... something else, why would shifters, especially wolves, hang with humans and other animals? I thought wolves were pack animals. Three or four hardly seems like a pack."

Taylor was drawing on every movie she'd watched and book she'd read as well as her knowledge. She didn't want to sit in blatant disbelief of Cass, but she didn't want to exactly feed into her ideas.

"First, there are a lot of misconceptions about wild wolves in mainstream media. We've changed their nature to fit our stories. Just like we do every other animal. Second, what we know about shifters, you said yourself, comes from movies and books. What if that's all bullshit? Made up to entertain us, just like every other thing about movies. I mean, it's an entertainment-driven industry, but the bottom line is to make money, and to do that, you have to make up the best story."

"You have a point there."

Shit.

"What about your mom? She would've shouted it from the rooftops or used it to manipulate your dad. She's a—and I'm only quoting you, not calling her this myself—ruthless bitch."

While Taylor agreed with that assessment one hundred and ten percent, she would never, and has never, badmouthed *that woman* to her daughter's face. Even though she heard from Cass that Allie didn't have the same boundary about her or anyone with tits who was even remotely connected to Prowler.

Cass talked enough shit about her mom that she didn't need, or really want, Taylor's agreement. She just needed a sounding board who wasn't her dad.

Cass just rolled her eyes.

"True, that was a sticking point for me too. I have to believe that it came about sometime after they broke up."

Taylor studied Cass for a moment. She really believed what she was saying. The last thing

Taylor wanted do was to discount her right off the bat. But somehow, she needed to give Prowler a heads-up but not totally dime Cass out. That would be a fine line to walk.

"Here." She handed Taylor the notebook. "Just read it with an open mind. If by our next overnight you don't have even the smallest suspicion, I'll drop it. Deal?"

"Only if you promise to keep an open mind to other possible explanations."

"Deal," Cass agreed. The relief on her face was clear at Taylor's acceptance of the possibility. She may or may not have mentally patted herself on the back a little for the way she handled it.

"Now, *Tombstone*?"

Rewinding, they watched the Earps arrive in Tombstone. They'd just started really paying attention to the movie when there was a knock at the door.

Taylor looked through the peephole and got the shock of her life. Her brother Travis stood on the other side.

Cautiously, she opened the door. Last time she'd seen him, he and her ex were tearing up the town and spending all her money. How the hell did he even find her? She opened the door just enough to stick her face out.

"I'm guessing I have Terry to thank for this unexpected and unwanted visit?" she grated through her teeth. Yeah, her older brother was the only way Travis could've found her. Fuck.

"Awww, is that any way to treat your brother, sis? You not going to invite me in for a cuppa?"

"When hell freezes over. What do you want?"

"Can't I just want to see my sister?"

"No. How much?" She didn't want to give him money, but if she didn't, he wouldn't leave. Then he'd spot Cass, and well, she'd be damned if that perv would set eyes on her.

"What makes—"

"How much, Travis? Name a number right fucking now or leave empty-handed, your choice."

"Whatever you got in cash, plus 5K? Check's okay."

Of course, a check was okay, the loser. Taylor closed and locked the door before grabbing her purse and emptying her wallet. Then, she hastily scrawled a check from the stash she kept in the entryway table.

With those in hand, she called back to Cass. "I'll be right outside. Back in a flash."

Stepping onto the porch and closing the door behind her, before locking it with the thumb sensor, she thrust the cash and check into his hand.

"That's it. Don't come back. Forget my address and the fact that I even exist."

"Taylor Norton, huh?"

"Forget that name, Travis."

"Awww, I love you too, sis," he said sarcastically before throwing his arms around her. He picked her up until her feet were off the ground. Then he kissed her on the lips in an unbrotherly fashion, catching her off guard.

Like father, like son.

He immediately turned and jogged down the steps.

She looked over toward Prowler's place before stepping back inside. Whoever was watching his place threw up his hand and waved.

Great.

3

PROWLER

Last night's visit and run had been intense. Not only did Hunter not look good at all, but they'd almost gotten caught in their fur.

Some fucking kids out riding dune buggies at night like morons.

They could've probably gotten away with a wolf here or there, but Monster, for one, didn't look natural in shifted form.

Plus, how could anyone explain a bear and a mountain lion hanging with some very odd-looking wolves? It just didn't make sense in the Nevada desert.

His first thought had been of Cass. What if something happened to him? She'd be left with just Allie and the endless string of men she brought into their lives. He didn't want that for his daughter.

Maybe it was time to think about settling down. Not just for him, but for Cass. She needed more stability in her life.

If Prowler officially took an ol' lady, he was positive he could get rid of Allie with enough of a payday. Allie harbored the notion of their getting back together one day. If he severed that hope for good, maybe she'd let him buy her off.

The more he thought about it, the more it made sense. He didn't know why he'd fought it for so long. Actually, he did know. It wasn't just once bitten, twice shy, although that was part of it.

No, the biggest obstacle was him, or rather a very furry part that lived deep inside of him.

Kansas was fairly sure that the instincts and drives of his wolf weren't as integrated as in naturals.

That was the information they were going with even though Kansas's information was limited. It was not as limited as his. Not to mention, in the quantum wolves, none of them had experienced the drives that Kansas did, at least not with the same intensity.

Prowler was still mulling all this over in his head as he strode into the chapel.

Something about the room always calmed him. Maybe it was the warm wood walls and furniture, accented by dark rich colors that were reminiscent of old gentlemen's clubs. Perhaps it was the gavel that had slammed down the well-deserved sentence of an infamous serial killer, and now rested innocently against the mahogany table that dominated the space.

Prowler was sure those things contributed to the feelings that washed over him, but the over-whelming sense of brotherhood and belonging told him it was the purpose of the space more than anything else.

It was where his shifter status took a backseat to his club.

His family.

Church didn't start for another fifteen minutes, so he sat in contemplative silence until Bulldog strode in with two steaming mugs of coffee, handing one to Prowler.

"Thank fuck." He took a sip and let the caffeine speak to his soul. "Did I ever tell you that you're my best VP ever?"

"I'm your only VP, dickbag."

"That doesn't invalidate the previous statement." He saluted him with his mug before taking another fortifying sip.

Their runs always wore them out. They only took fur once a week or less, depending on who needed it the most. So, packing a week's worth of running and hunting into one night was exhausting.

Without thinking, Prowler blurted out what had been on his mind. A question he'd meant to pose only to himself, but he kinda just asked Bulldog.

"Do you think it's possible for men like us to settle down?"

"If you mean Kings who don't exactly follow the letter of the law, yeah, with the right woman. If you mean shifters, then, well, also yeah, with the right woman. But if you mean you and me specifically? Me, of course, I'm just a cuddly ol' teddy bear and emotionally available if I need to be. If you mean you, well, she'd have to be one hell of a woman who'd probably still get tired of your shit after a while. You are possibly the most emotionally unavailable fucker I know, and I spent my formative years with my father, so that's saying something."

"Wow, next time don't sugarcoat it."

"Fuck that. You want sugar, go grab a fucking Snickers. You want honesty, well ..." He gestured to himself with his mug before taking another sip.

He knew Bulldog was no-nonsense. That was probably why his brain told his mouth to speak aloud.

"You think I'm emotionally unavailable?"

His veep spewed coffee over the table.

"Emotionally unavailable is the understatement of the century. Here's regular fuckers over here." Bulldog gestured with his mug all the way to the left. "And emotionally unavailable is over here." He gestured with his right hand. "You are over there by that fucking wall somewhere." He pointed.

"Point made." With that kind of glowing assessment, there wasn't much to be gained by continuing the conversation, but Bulldog had other ideas.

"Here's the thing though, Prez, I believe you're only in a state of forced unavailability. I bet before the ex and the wolf, you were *too* available. The all-in type of guy who expected the house with a picket fence and a golden retriever or some shit. Am I right?"

Prowler didn't answer, he didn't need to.

"So, this." He reached for Prowler's empty mug. "Is all a suit of armor, not your true nature."

Bulldog disappeared, then returned with full mugs.

So maybe there was a point in continuing. Bulldog had hit the nail on the head. If he were honest with himself, he wanted to get somewhat back to who he'd once been. He missed that part of himself to an extent. The question was how to do that.

So much was at stake already, more so if he added the people he cared about.

If he went to jail on club business, it would mean leaving a family while he did his time. With the life they led, prison time was a real possibility.

If he ever went inside, he'd have to sever with his wolf, like Hunter. Hunter hadn't been the same since and would never be the same. Even if he got out, his life would be just a shell. The only blessing is that the club was his only family. He didn't have an ol' lady visiting on Saturdays or crying at home for her man who wasn't coming home.

But Prowler had Cass. At least she was fourteen now, and maybe if he got an ol' lady, she could look out for Cass.

That thought brought other potential problems to his pipe dream.

"How would I even begin to explain the wolf to a woman?" The wolf in question gave a menacing growl that faded into a whimper. Prowler didn't know what it meant. All the years together, and he still couldn't communicate with his wolf as well as naturals.

"*A* woman or a *specific* woman?"

Prowler just eyed his VP. Bulldog knew exactly who had Prowler asking those questions, and it wasn't just for his daughter, no matter how he tried to convince himself otherwise.

He just stared at Bulldog rather than answer.

"That particular woman can handle all that and then some. However—"

"However, what?"

Prowler sat up straighter, leaning over the table, waiting for the *however*.

"You two exclusive?" Why was he asking shit like that?

"No, and yes." With that mumbled answer, he relaxed back against his chair. It bothered him to no end that he hadn't gotten more than a *we will end it when we want to bang other people* agreement on their little arrangement.

"Care to elaborate on that, Prez?"

"Not really. However, what?"

"Boogey said there was a man at her place last night."

Prowler shot out of the chair as if his ass were on fire.

"What?"

He wasn't just pissed that Taylor was entertaining another man, but that his daughter was there. That was a line, one that although she didn't know existed, she'd crossed. With everything Taylor knew about Allie and the men in and out of Cass's life, he couldn't imagine why she'd have thought that would be okay.

"Calm down, Prez. From what was captured on the camera footage, he never entered the residence. She made him wait outside, and when she slipped out the door, she did so with just enough room to clear her rack before closing it behind her. Then she handed him something, he pocketed it, picked her up, gave her a kiss, and left. The whole exchange lasted about three minutes."

Prowler wiggled his fingers toward his vice until he pulled his phone from his pocket and cued up the footage. After turning up the brightness, Prowler watched the man walk up from down the street.

The asshole jogged up the porch, rang, knocked, and rang again before Taylor opened the door a sliver and stuck her face through. A few seconds later, she closed the door, while the man shoved his hands into his pockets and rocked back and forth on his heels, waiting.

When Taylor emerged again, closing the door behind her, she handed him something, then crossed her arms. Looking behind her at the door before turning back to the man. Sure enough, after pocketing whatever she gave him, he scooped her into his arms and kissed her on the lips.

Lips he would give his left nut to kiss but had held off doing so. One, because kissing was way too intimate for hookups. And two, he feared that as with natural wolves, he would know immediately if they belonged together.

Kansas said he'd get a sense of it, one Kansas hadn't experienced yet, but had been described to him by those who had, as a sense of peace and belonging. Home.

It wasn't unusual to see Kansas lock lips with

every chick in a bar. It was how he greeted people, always looking for the one to be his.

So, Prowler had avoided kissing since he'd learned that little tidbit. Truth be told, he wasn't afraid of kissing Taylor because she might be his mate, but instead because she might not be.

If he didn't sense anything at all, he was afraid he'd always wonder if his mate was still out there or if quantum wolves, as they'd taken to calling it, were just missing that drive like some of the other instincts naturals had.

Always wondering if there was someone out there that his wolf might fall for would kill a relationship. That's the real reason he hadn't kissed Taylor. It was like Schrödinger's cat. She was and wasn't his mate at the same time, as long as he never kissed her.

But the man in the video didn't have that issue. Prowler wanted to throw the phone across the room and go find Taylor. Pin her against the nearest surface and erase that man's lips from hers with his own. He also wanted to throw the phone across the room, end things with Taylor, and grab one of the girls working for them and fuck her into next week.

Was Taylor ready to end their agreement and

just hadn't seen him yet to tell him? Or was she going to string two men along for however long it benefited her?

He didn't think she was that type, which is why he even took up with her to begin with. However, he didn't think he'd catch his ex in reverse cowgirl with another man when he married her either.

He was so deep in his head that he hadn't realized all his brothers were there and waiting for him to open their meeting until Bulldog cleared his throat.

Prowler pulled his head out of his ass, dropped the gavel, and went immediately into discussing Hunter and Sleeper. Normally he liked to clear out old business first and handle shifter business after church, but Hunter wasn't doing well, and this time, shifter and club business were intertwined.

Everyone looked to Kansas, the resident shifter expert, or what passed for one, for input.

"Like I said before, the only people I knew who suppressed their wolves with silver-laced tattoos all eventually went crazy or died, but it seems to be happening a lot quicker in Hunter than in the other cases I've seen."

They all knew it was coming because, fuck if Kansas didn't tell them that from the jump.

Suppress wasn't the most accurate word. Severing the connection between man and beast was a more apt term. Other than killing Hunter, it was the only choice they had. He would be locked away for a long time no matter what, and he couldn't last more than a month or two before his wolf forced a change.

"I think the difference is the tatt. In the men I knew about, it was redone, or more were added, every few years. The collective theory was when the wolf tries to break through and can't, that's when it drives the man over the edge. So, keeping the wolf quiet is key. Of course, this was all still being tested when I left the commune."

Prowler had considered it himself, but they were unsure of how it would work in a quantum wolf, and he had Cass to consider.

As it was, they were two entities reluctantly sharing space. Natural wolves talked to their man, and they melded, two halves of a whole, but quantums were apparently different.

In the last few months, though, something had changed between Prowler and his wolf. He was growling and howling more, but Prowler still couldn't decipher him.

"So, if we can smuggle in some silver-laced ink or powdered silver, we may buy him a few more years at a time," Boogeyman mused.

"Worth a shot. The biggest issue with prison ink is infection. Does the severed wolf also suppress his wolf immunity and healing?" Monster asked.

"I don't know. That wasn't brought up before I left."

Prowler didn't miss the look that raced across Kansas's face. He'd left because the pricks in his community were testing on their own kind. Kansas found out that it wasn't a voluntary program when they came for him. He was running away from other wolves, and Prowler was trying to run away from his own when they found each other.

They loved motorcycles and spent all their free time either on two wheels or four paws.

Before long, Bulldog, Ghoul, and Monster had joined them, and their chapter of the Kings of Anarchy MC was born.

"I can try to see if my friend is still there and if

he has any information, but no promises. It's been over a decade."

For Kansas to volunteer to call anyone from his old pack was proof that his loyalty and love for his brothers in the Kings far outweighed the hatred for the Green Tree Commune, a.k.a. the Domino Pack.

The pack had killed Kansas's whole family by the time he'd turned twenty-five. A family he thought died for a cause, the greater good, voluntarily. But in reality, they died to make a so-called alpha rich.

"Infection is the least of our worries. It's a risk we need to take—ASAP," Prowler decided. "Ghoul, call the Shadow Angels Prez and make it happen. We need to get silver inside sooner rather than later. Give her a marker." Prowler hated owing anyone a favor, but Ripley had a direct line into the prison, one they needed, and her club's only restrictions were drugs or weapons, and their favor was neither of those things.

Ghoul lived at the Angels-owned trailer park and so was their "direct line" to the prison. Prowler had considered, more than once, letting Ghoul cut out the middlewoman, but he didn't need bad blood. Their clubs co-existed peacefully in the same city, so why fuck that up?

"It's as good as done."

After a few more housekeeping things and financial reports, it came time for his least favorite subject, loan jumpers.

"Travis Barton is behind again. This is the third time. Last few times it was a matter of hours, so no need to call in muscle. This time he was a week late when we sent Chef and Monster to talk to him, now he's in the wind." Kansas reports.

"Anything to add?" Prowler turned to Chef and Monster.

"Real prick. At first, said he'd have it in a week, so we gave him a reminder of what a week had already cost him and what another would tack on. As he drove off, he yelled some shit, but it's nothing anyone else doesn't say when we come a-knocking."

"Word on the street is he's been running his mouth, bragging about stiffing us," Monster added.

"Any clue where to start looking?" Prowler knew if they had any answers, they would've said, but he asked anyway.

"His SRO was cleaned out. His car tags

expired. Parents deceased. Two siblings. A sister who fell off the face of the earth a few years ago. Only viable lead is a brother over in Utah."

"What's the damage?"

"Fifteen."

"Loan or in-house?"

Most people would assume that a fifteen-thousand-dollar debt was just that, but the Kings treated it differently. If they lent 15K in cash, that was a lot worse than someone who gambled away that same amount on credit at the Kings' tables.

A cash loan came with much higher interest, but both still had to be paid back so others didn't get ideas. Besides, Travis was running his mouth, and that had to be dealt with.

"He split it. Took ten in-house and walked with the other five."

The Kings didn't like to make noise unless they needed to. All loans went through their check-cashing business to clean shit up, but if someone looked too hard into their loan practices, there'd be questions.

"Get some more info on the brother. Mainly what he does and who he knows. Then we'll find the angle to come at the brother to find Travis and get our money back from him one way or another."

What Prowler didn't have to say was hands off the brother. They weren't in the habit of transferring responsibility to any available party. Now, if said party was aware that Travis owed them and was hiding him, that was a different story.

"What else we got?"

"Got the ride through Red Rock next week and the party at Ransom after. The noise waiver came through this week, but we had a snafu with the food truck, but I'm on it. I'll keep you informed."

Prowler nodded. They needed new blood, so a party was what was called for. However, some of their animals felt territorial over their clubhouse, so when they hosted a more public event, one where every single attendee wasn't vetted, they opted for the bar.

They cordoned off the parking lot, hired a band, and kept it always lit. Bonus, the hotel reaped the benefits of overindulgence with their discounted room rates for ticket holders. Plus, it was always good for scoping out potential customers for their brothel and tables.

After all other business and issues had been addressed, Prowler gaveled the meeting closed. He wanted nothing more than to get home to his daughter and see Taylor.

He wasn't sure if he was pissed at her or not, nor was he sure if they should end things or keep going. What he did know was, either way, their relationship had to change. He just wasn't sure which way that would be yet.

The hard part was Taylor would have to wait. Cassidy came first, and his time with her was limited.

Just then the air was filled with an old Le Tigre and Bunny song.

"You changed my ringtone again, I see."

Her laughter was lively. "Do you like it?"

"Better than the last one, I guess. What's up, Jellybean?"

The last song had been some country singer from like the fifties, so yeah, "The Cars That Go Boom" was better.

"What time will you be home tonight?"

"Around five. What do you want me to pick up on the way home? Lettuce or tomatoes?" he joked.

"Ugh, Dad, you know vegan food is more ... never mind. Don't pick up anything except some wildflowers. And maybe spray some cologne on before you head home so you don't smell like, well, smoke, sweat, and perfume."

The last word was said with an upward inflection combined with a conspiratorial tone. He didn't exactly hide what he did from Cass, but he didn't share details either. She knew the club owned businesses, the legit ones, anyway, but apparently, she smelled the not-so-legal ones on him as well.

"Why?" Then some pieces fell into place. "Cass, this smells like a setup." One that he didn't exactly hate the idea of.

"Taylor ordered this vegan tenderloin that finally arrived, and we're making beefless wellington. It'll be nice, and maybe you guys can get to know each other over dessert."

"I thought you had a rule that I couldn't look at anyone you considered a friend, no matter their age?"

"Dad." He could practically hear her eyes roll. "Tay is different, and ..." His daughter trailed off.

"And what?"

If he knew his daughter, he could hear that she had a lot to say.

"And, well, she deserves ... nothing, Dad. Just don't be like my uncles, okay?"

Two things jumped out at him. One, his daughter was holding back, and two, as much as he tried to keep the club activities from touching his daughter, he'd failed.

"What do you mean, like your uncles? They're good men. You know that. Just a little rough around the edges sometimes."

He had zero doubt about how much she loved them, and they loved her, but did she really know way more than he'd believed? Was he being that naïve?

"I know that, Dad. They're great in fact, including you, but they go through girlfriends like I do clean socks."

Prowler dropped his head into his hand. Fuck, he was that naïve to think that he could hide his lifestyle from his ridiculously smart daughter.

Another thought crept in ... if she knew more about the club than he'd expected, did she also know more about them? More specifically, a certain side of them?

On her last visit, Cass had mentioned living more of the time with him than with Allie. Since then, he had been considering it, mulling over the best way to make that happen but keep his life, specifically shifter and club issues, from touching her. Lord knew he'd have her twenty-four seven if he could.

Maybe it was time to sit down and have a serious talk with his daughter, since she was now playing pint-sized matchmaker. If she figured it out on her own, it could be dangerous, especially if she told someone else.

"What do you say we drive out to the lake tomorrow and rent a boat? Just you and me. Father-daughter time."

Her squealed, "Yes," had him pulling the phone away from his ear. "I'd love that, Dad. There are some things I've been wanting to talk to you about," she added in a nervous tone.

Ditto, kid, ditto, he thought.

The rest of his day flew by with that weight lifted off him. He made a run by the brothel and bar just to check on operations and spent an hour in the table room. Then took a courtesy call from a club passing through for the weekend.

Even though he kept busy, his mind wandered back to Taylor. After Cass went to sleep, he planned on getting her underneath him. Fuck the guy on her porch. Fuck the wolf and a chosen mate. And fuck ending what they had going. Why not go for it? If he was going to have an ol' lady, it would be his sexy neighbor or no one at all.

Parking in his garage, he pulled the bundle of wildflowers from his saddlebag before stepping into what smelled like the wrong house.

He loved his daughter, but he wasn't on board with her vegan lifestyle, except when she was around. He would do anything for her, including giving up steak around her, but the house didn't smell like tofu at the moment. Nope, it smelled like good old-fashioned grade A beef.

"Dad." Cass was first to spot him. With her greeting, Taylor turned away from the stove where it looked like she was plating asparagus.

"Hi, Prowler," she said with a blush. One that made him wonder if she was thinking the same thing he was. About their last encounter, when he'd hauled her over his shoulder to the garage and fucked her bent over the tank of his bike as they both straddled the seat.

Hell, he got hard every time he threw his leg over it picturing her there before him. Glistening pink pussy as he pummeled in and out of her.

"Look, Tay, Dad brought you flowers."

Taylor turned, wiping her hands and hefting the plate, heading toward the table.

"I think those are for you, Cass," she said with certainty, like he'd never in a million years bring her flowers.

If they stood any chance of taking this beyond fucking, he needed to alter her perception.

"Actually." He separated the two distinct bouquets. "You're both right." He handed the smaller one that was dip-dyed in bright colors to Cass, dropping a kiss on the top of her head. "These are for my favorite girl in the world."

He approached Taylor, who was looking more like she was expecting to be handed a live rattlesnake instead of flowers. "And these." He handed her the larger collection of daisies and black-eyed Susans before looking back to see that Cass was turned away. He leaned in, trailing a finger down her bare bicep, and pitched his voice low. "Are for my favorite woman in the world."

Taylor jerked back to stare at him. Her face was not the happy reaction he'd expected, but instead a narrow-eyed suspicious one.

"Um, thanks. Sit, eat." She bolted to the kitchen. "I'm not feeling very good, so I'm going to, um, just go. You two enjoy dinner."

"Taylor, please don't go." The heartbreak in his daughter's voice almost killed him. It was clear he'd fucked up, but he didn't have a clue as to how, but he would fix it.

Seeing Cass looking sad and Taylor looking like a wounded kitten made him realize the truth in his earlier words.

They *were* his two favorite people, and somehow, he'd cluelessly hurt them both.

Fuck.

4

TAYLOR

"No, Tay. Stay. You did all this work. Even ordered vegan stuff for me, when I know you'd rather eat the real thing, so please?" Cass's sweet begging face was impossible to resist. When she glanced up, Prowler looked apologetic, even though neither one knew what was going on in her head.

Apparently, being given flowers was still a trigger she hadn't realized was still a trigger. Every time her dad had boundary issues, he'd apologize with flowers. Then, the first time her brother followed his pattern, complete with apologies and flowers, she got the fuck out of that toxic environment, even though it had meant sleeping in her piece of shit car for months. It was still a far sight better than staying at home.

Then it was from one bad situation to another until she finally got the courage to end it once and for all. The trigger then had been, yep, flowers. Hospital flowers were always worse than acute care flowers for some reason. Maybe because it made her feel so much more stupid because of the severity of it all. So, when Billy went to jail, it was the wilting flowers that whispered to her it was time to go.

However, there was no need to make Cass, or even Prowler, pay for someone else's or multiple someone else's sins. Taylor was a work in progress, so she decided to see the flowers as a step in that journey.

"Of course, sorry, I just let my mind go somewhere else for a hot minute. I'm gonna put these in water so they don't wilt." She plastered a smile on her face, one she knew she'd start to feel the longer she spent with Prowler and Cass.

After placing hers and Cass's flowers in water, they all sat at the table. Prowler reached over and took the knife and serving fork from her with a smile.

When their eyes met, her stomach did a little flutter. His denim-blue eyes stared at her with softness and questions. It took her aback. Prowler had always reserved his softness for Cass. Sometimes she envied it, if she were being honest. Being on the receiving end of it was dizzying. Maybe it was just the emotional aftermath she was in that was doing it.

She put both her hands in her lap to resist the urge to reach up and stroke his soft blond beard. One she knew the feel of against almost every inch of her skin.

Just the thought had her pulse racing and core heating. "Jellybean, will you grab a soda for Taylor?"

She heard the scrape of the chair and Cass's retreating steps but couldn't look away. Prowler's probing gaze held her captive. When he spoke, his voice seemed a little huskier than normal, like when they —

"Taylor." He leaned into her, nipping her neck where it sloped into her shoulder, right where he knew turned her legs to pudding. Nothing could hold back the moan that escaped her. "If you keep looking at me like that, I'll throw you over my shoulder and be balls deep inside you before we have dessert."

A whimper left her mouth as he stood back upright and began slicing the Wellington as

Cassidy placed an unopened can of soda by her plate and sat down.

Without a thought, she reached for the can and rolled the cool exterior along her heated neck. A choked sound escaped Prowler as he sliced.

Instead of looking at him, Taylor turned to Cass to try to divert her attention. The kid was too perceptive by far.

"So, um, how's your social studies project coming along?"

Cass had talked to her in depth about it, and Taylor thought it was a great idea. Cass's big fear was that her dad might not agree, so Taylor decided to open the subject for them.

"Oh, you've decided what you're doing it on then?" Prowler asked.

Taylor was a little proud of herself for that flawless segway.

Their plates were loaded down, and everyone had taken at least one bite before Cass spoke.

"Yeah. I've decided to explore the relationship impacts between family and friends when one person goes vegan."

Prowler choked a little on his Wellington before furrowing his brow. Taylor wanted to reach over and smooth the wrinkles away. He was sexy even when he wasn't doing anything remotely sexy, and that didn't bode well for her chances of ending their arrangement, but she needed to. She was in too deep already, and he wasn't the settling down type. Fuck, she wasn't either, at least not until those thoughts started creeping in over the last week or so. Hell, the no-strings part of their relationship was why she'd been so stoked about the whole proposal.

What is it they say about the best-laid plans? Yeah, that. The more intimate they were, the deeper she fell, and the deeper she fell, the more she wanted exclusivity, and that was just a hair's breadth from all-out commitment in her mind.

Forcing herself to bring up the picture of his ex-wife's lips on his did the trick. She ate in silence as they spoke about Cass's idea.

"What relationship changes? I don't think it's a big deal. You're vegan, I'm not, but we love each other all the same."

Prowler spoke with such matter-of-fact authority, as if Cass wouldn't be able to have a single thing to say to that. But Taylor knew better. Cass had laid it all out for her before, and she got exactly what Cass was putting down.

"I don't mean it the way you think I mean it.

Well, not completely. Of course, everyone still loves everyone else. I mean little things, like the fact that you hide your bacon double cheeseburger noshing from me when I visit, even though you know that I know you eat them. Why? Is it because you feel judged by me?"

The sincerity and worry in Cass's voice was tugging at her heart. Cass had explained it all before, but knowing that she picked the project because she really was worried about her dad's feelings was next level.

Especially since she thought he was ... Oh, shit. It just hit her like a speeding locomotive. The sly little shit, it wasn't all about veganism. It was also a metaphor for the possibility of her dad being a shifter and hiding that.

Fuck, Taylor was so dick drunk for Prowler that she'd totally forgotten that conversation from last night.

Fuck.

Fuck.

Fuck.

"No, Cass. Never. You have never made me feel anything but love." He put his fork down and raked his fingers through his blond locks. "You give me more joy than anything in my life ever has or ever will. Period."

"Then why do you hide it from me? Why not just do it right out in the open? Let me see you for who you are." She crossed her arms over her chest, adopting the same haughty look Prowler did when he thought he had someone cornered. Those two were so much alike it was scary.

Taylor cut her eyes to Prowler's, and where she normally saw denim blue, there was a flash of gold. It happened so fast, it had to be a trick of the light.

"Because I always want to make you proud. There are parts of me ... I mean ... my life that I know wouldn't do that, so I just ... eat that before I come home to you."

Prowler seemed flustered. His speech halted as if tripping over his words. That was new. He was almost always composed.

Cass looked Taylor's way and raised an eyebrow as if to say, *see*.

"That's an impact. A small one, but still." Cass continued to eat as if this was the most casual conversation in the world. And while she was obviously using it as a metaphor—at least it seemed obvious now—she was also passionate in a way only the young can be. Taylor had to admire her. Cass thought she could save the world. And fuck if her confidence didn't make Taylor want to see her do it.

"Take my friends, well, friend, for example. If she is going out to eat, she never invites me along anymore, and we've grown apart. She says it's because she knows I won't want to go, but that's not true. I'd go all the time and just have a salad. The true reason is either she feels judged by me, even though I make it a point to say absolutely nothing, or she doesn't want me around because she feels bad about eating animals when I'm there. So, see? Impacts."

Cass sounded devastated about growing apart from her best friend Misha.

Taylor kept her thoughts to herself. This was their discussion, but she paid attention to the dynamic between them and the words exchanged.

Even with a topic that obviously made Prowler uncomfortable, it was clear he enjoyed talking to his kid. Not just going through the motions but engaging with her and truly listening.

It shouldn't have been as big of a turn-on as it was since Taylor had zero desire to have her own children, but God help her, it was.

As their conversation hit a lull, Taylor excused herself to retrieve dessert.

After giving them each a plate with a vegan carob brownie, Taylor took a pass. Not because it didn't look absolutely amazing, but because she was working hard to cut out sweets, her kryptonite.

"This looks great, Tay." Cass's compliment slid into her heart. "Don't you think so too, Dad?"

She swallowed back a groan at the obvious matchmaking and gave Cass a look that said, *knock it off.*

"Umhm," Prowler answered as he took a huge bite. No sooner did it go in than it was spewing out. Cass was a bit more subtle, but the end result was all the same. The brownie went in, and the brownie came immediately back out.

"Oh my god, what's wrong?" Her first thought was a classic sitcom mix-up with salt and sugar, but the vegan recipe called for agave, so that wasn't it.

"It's um..." She waited for Prowler to finish, but he didn't. Just guzzled soda like his throat was on fire.

"What?"

"It's fucking awful," Cass said.

Both turned to her and scolded, "Language."

"Sorry, but it's true," she reiterated as she in turn gulped her drink.

"She's not exaggerating," Prowler quipped. Taylor's cheeks were on fire. She wasn't on board with the whole setup vibe of the night, but neither was she ready to be embarrassed.

"No wonder she's not having any. She pranked us." Cass was obviously joking. Prowler's laughter joined his daughters. That took a little sting out of it, but not all.

"I followed the recipe to the letter. It took me forever to track down carob, which I'd never even heard of." She crossed her arms over her chest like a petulant child. It didn't escape her notice that Prowler's gaze dropped to her cleavage almost instantly. Good. It's hard to laugh when distracted.

"That's the problem. You followed a recipe, which I can only assume was written by hippies in a commune in the mid-seventies."

"I don't get it. What do hippies have to do with anything?"

Taylor didn't have a clue what Prowler meant by that.

"What is fu..." Cass looked over the top of her

phone with a raised eyebrow. "Fudging carob?" Cass whispered as she typed. If the vegan didn't know, then Taylor definitely went wrong somewhere.

"According to the internet, it's a flowering evergreen shrub in the subfamily of a legume." She reads more before proclaiming. "It's supposedly like chocolate, but dogs can eat it."

With that announcement, she grabbed her plate and stood. "Let's skip dessert next time if you wanna feed us dog chocolate."

Taylor was powerless to hold back her laughter.

"I second that," Prowler agreed.

"Ouch, shots fired." Taylor gripped her chest where the imaginary wound was. "But valid. Agreed, no more carob."

"I'm going to call it a night and go listen to music in my room." With that, Cass winked, freaking winked, and in the same manner as her dad, no less. After dropping her plate in the sink, Cass slid her headphones from her neck to her ears. "Loudly." She added and disappeared into her room.

Once gone, Prowler reached for Taylor's arms, which were still crossed over her chest. He interlaced their fingers and rested their joined hands on the table.

"Thanks for trying with Cass. It means a lot … to her." The last two words sounded like an afterthought. Like it meant a lot to him, but he chose not to reveal that.

She wished.

"Of course, you know I adore her."

Prowler's inhale was audible. "And to me. It means a lot to me too." The way he said it was forced but sincere. Almost as if voicing gratitude was foreign to him.

Taylor just smiled and cleared the table.

She didn't do well with emotions, especially unexpected ones … and from the man she'd fallen for when she'd promised she wouldn't.

She started rinsing and loading the dishes to keep from blurting out, *I think I kinda love you, and Cass thinks you're a werewolf.*

Strong, tattooed arms wrapped around her from behind, removing the plate from her hand and setting it in the sink.

"What? No, *of course I adore you too*, for me?"

"You know you're too handsome for your own good." She turned in his embrace to face him.

"Look at you. Do you really need your ego stroked that much?"

"Too handsome for my own good, huh?"

Taylor rolled her eyes.

Dipping his head, he nibbled her neck in that perfect spot again. He seemed to be fascinated with it, and she didn't mind. Fuck, the man knew how to turn her bones into jelly.

"Besides, the thought of you stroking anything of mine is fucking appealing."

"Ugh." She pushed him away gently and turned to finish the dishes.

Taylor was flustered ... he flustered her. She needed to talk to him about Cass without exactly talking to him about Cass and what she thought.

Sadly, that was the second thing on her to-do list that seemed almost impossible. Especially with his lips on her neck or when he was doing domestic shit. Like rinsing dishes as he was now.

Gazing to the side, she watched the movement of his tattooed forearms, and he waved the plate under the stream of water.

Something about a sexy biker doing what old white men called *women's work* was sexy as fuck.

Taylor didn't realize she was staring at him with

her mouth agape until Prowler pulled the soapy dessert plate from her iron grip with a grin. His other hand lifted her bottom jaw with a single finger.

Shamelessly, she took one step aside and just watched him finish the dishes by himself.

Taylor unabashedly appreciated the scene before her. She thought the man looked fine as hell in his cut and thick-soled boots. Black Henley underneath, looking every inch the stereotypical outlaw.

However, there was a lot to be said about him without the cut or boots. His bare feet poked out from the bottom of his jeans. There wasn't a woman alive who wouldn't appreciate the way his shirt clung to his muscles, but when he'd pushed those sleeves up his arms? Damn if he didn't jump fifty points on the *fuck me, daddy* meter.

What was on her to-do list again?

At some point, Prowler finished the dishes by himself and pulled her into his arms. "Should we take this down the hall?"

Down the hall?

Yes, wait, no.

"But ..." Shit, she wanted to forget why she was supposed to protest, at least for the next hour or so.

"Cassidy." Her name trailed off as Prowler nipped his way across her collarbone. Fuck, why was she making excuses? She should either get on with it or enjoy one last night of passion before she ended things.

"What about her?" He spoke between kisses and nips and kisses and nips. "Did you not get the memo that this was a setup?"

Kisses and nips. Fuck, his mouth was fire, leaving a trail of scorched skin in its wake.

"And we don't want to disappoint her, do we?" The humor in his voice almost overpowered the lust ... almost.

Taylor couldn't help but smile. Giving in to at least a little heavy petting, she stroked her hands up his chest under his shirt.

An animalistic growl escaped his lips. That roughness in his voice practically stroked her clit and erased her memory. There was a reason she needed to say no, or at least press pause, but for the life of her, she couldn't recall it. Actually, she could remember; she just chose to have selective memory ... just for tonight.

"But ... but what if she—"

"Hears?" He pulled back to ask. Taylor was only capable of nodding before he tossed her over his shoulder and strode down the hall. "Head-phones, loud, remember?"

Right, so Cassidy was taken care of. But something else, or multiple something elses, weren't. With his lips off her, reason returned. She really should rip it off like a Band-Aid and end the intimate nature of their relationship.

But Taylor was realizing that when it came to Prowler, she was selfish. She wanted more, and since she couldn't have more, she'd take tonight. No guilt, no heartbreak. Just a beautiful goodbye to the way things had been.

When he deposited her on his bed with a bounce and ripped his shirt over his head, a moan escaped her lips. That's what she needed to get out of her head and enjoy this last night of mind-blowing sex.

While it would be so much more for her.

She leaned up on her elbows and cataloged the play of every muscle as he stripped down to nothing. The only distraction was the sound of a marble or two hitting the floor. She made a mental note to ask him why he carried them but was distracted when his cock jumped. Fuck if he wasn't a goddamn fictional character.

Ropes of muscle under gallons of ink. Muscles

that flexed as he took the few steps to the foot of the bed in slow motion, like he was prowling.

Prowler prowling. She barely stifled her laugh.

Taylor's eyes swept down his body to his feet, which again she found attractive, and she hated feet. It was strange how she viewed Prowler through a different lens from all other men.

Maybe that's why she'd fallen for him. She removed the goggles that protected her from the heartbreak she'd donned after Billy.

When he was mere inches from the mattress, he stopped and held his arms out. "Like what you see, babe?" Taking a step back, he stood there with zero shame as she drank in his body.

Hell yeah, she liked what she saw, a little too much. Continuing her perusal, her gaze slowly rose up to his thighs, which were thick and defined. There was a furrow that ran down the outside and curved inward. Whatever muscle that outlined, it was sexy as hell.

While his thighs distracted her for a moment, it was what was just north of there that demanded her attention.

Prowler's delicious ... and highly addictive ... cock.

As beautiful a sight as it was, standing proud

and primed, she wanted to see all of him ... remember all of him.

A spin of her finger was all it took for him to do exactly what that slutty little voice in her head wanted.

"Damn that ass."

When he flexed his hard cheeks, she realized she'd spoken aloud.

He turned back around and lazily stroked his cock while staring at her with his oh-so-blue eyes.

A team of the top sculptors in the world, working around the clock for a decade, could try to sculpt a perfect specimen of a man from marble, and it still wouldn't hold a candle to Prowler.

"I think you're a little overdressed for the occasion."

Before the last syllable left his mouth, she'd pulled the shirt over her head and wiggled out of her pants.

Her mind came back online unbidden.

Sadness washed over her when she remembered, once again, that this was their last time.

A goodbye fuck.

She would miss so much about *them*. One of

the things was the comfortable and comical nature of their intimacy. She'd never had that.

Hell, if she had laughed about anything when her ex was naked, he would have lost his shit thinking she was laughing at him. Prowler wasn't insecure like that, and that alone was a turn on.

Taylor would give anything to continue on as they were, but she was in too deep. The neighbors-with-benefits arrangement had run its course.

Relationships with caps had a limited run time. They should be categorized more as entanglements.

Their agreement had reached the cap placed on it, so it was coming to a close, and the credits were rolling. It was either end it or advance it, and, well, they had been very clear on the possibility of advancement ... there wasn't one.

So, she planned to enjoy the *them* for one last night. After that aspect was dealt with, they could continue as friends. Friends who didn't sleep together but who had a connection based on the location of their homes and his daughter's care when he was unavailable.

Maybe in the coming week, over coffee ... in

public she could find a way to bring up Cass's beliefs. Safe mid-morning, non-sexual coffee.

Simple, just as Prowler had laid out in the beginning, when they both finally gave in to their desires.

Prowler's warm grasp on her ankles demanded attention. He placed her feet against his shoulders and dropped to his knees.

Taylor focused on every spot their bodies touched, down to the soles of her feet against his tattooed skin. She wanted to commit everything to long-term memory.

Normally, she simply laid back and enjoyed the bliss of riding his tongue, but today, she was staring down her stomach at the man who'd ruined her without even knowing it. He looked extra wicked, staring back when she could only see the top half of his face.

That weird trick-of-light eye thing happened again, but the room was dark. Hell, could it …? Was it poss—

Prowler's rough voice cut through her musings.

"My favorite place on the planet is right here." He spoke against her skin. "I love the view." Prowler nuzzled the sensitive skin of her inner thighs. She pretended for just a second that he'd replaced *the view* with you.

When he dove into her pussy tongue first, all thoughts of what he did and didn't say, and what she needed to say, fled.

He tongue-fucked her to oblivion and back before crawling up her body and scooting them both up the bed.

Prowler licked his lips, lips she'd never kissed, like he'd just eaten the most decadent dessert, definitely not carob. "Have I told you lately how much I love your taste?"

Again, with the word she longed to hear, but applied to a part of her, not her as a whole.

"Once or twice." She spoke a little more harshly than she should've as he rubbed the head of his cock against her clit.

If she took him into her body right then, she'd ninety-nine-point nine percent blurt out words of love too, but the kind that would have him ending everything. Not just the benefits part of their association, but likely everything. Hell, he'd probably pack up and move out of state.

Taylor had thought she was anti-relationship prior to meeting and fucking Prowler. He made her look like a commitment junkie compared to him. Prowler was to relationships as a vampire was to the sun.

Avoid and run.

Or so it had always seemed, but ... no. She wouldn't go there. She wouldn't read into things and let hope taint the way she perceived everything from his words to the way he looked into her eyes. No. She was stretching, and that was why it had to end. She would go insane grasping at straws, taking the crumbs he dropped, and making them into something they weren't, and it would destroy her.

Maybe if she'd ever had a single healthy relationship in her life, she could navigate the waters better, but she hadn't. Apparently she was all in or all out. She couldn't do casual. Since she was heading all in, she had to reverse course and go all out. The sadness was threatening to spill out, so she willed herself to take control of her emotions.

Wiggling her hips away from his probing cock, she pushed at his shoulders until he took the hint and rolled onto his back.

"Oh yeah, ride the shit out of me, babe. I love it when these tits are bouncing in my face." He growled as he kneaded her heavy breasts. When he pinched one nipple to the border of pain, she almost gave in and put him inside her. She was still too emotionally raw for that just yet.

"How about I suck your dick until you're ready to blow, then I let you fuck 'em?"

The instant shout of agreement that left his mouth practically rattled the walls. She knew how much he loved that.

Crawling down his body, she held the girls together and slid them up and down his length a few times to get him primed. The precum leaking from the head made the glide so much easier.

"Fuck, babe. Stop teasing me and put me in your mouth, or I'm taking over."

He always took over blow jobs. He almost never let her control it from start to finish. He loved them too much for that, but she loved how she could make him lose all control.

Before swallowing his length, she licked down the vein to his balls, sucking one, then the other into her mouth first. His growl signaled his patience was at its end, so she released his ball with a soft pop and gripped him at the base.

"Now, Tay. Fuck." Slamming his fists on the bed, his hips rocketed up the second her mouth closed around the head. She couldn't take as much of him like this, and they both knew it. "Babe."

Like a well-choreographed dance, she released him, and he jumped off the bed, pumping his dick impatiently as she positioned her head off the edge, elongating her throat.

No sooner had she opened her lips than he drove home. Pounding all seven inches in and out of her throat while rubbing his thumbs up and down the front of her neck in time with his thrusts.

Taylor only gagged a few times when his thrusts were faster than her swallowing. It was an art she'd perfected, thanks to, of all things, tips from an anesthesiologist student she'd hooked up with a few times.

"I'm about to blow, babe. Squeeze those tits for me." She complied, and as soon as she did, he pulled out from her throat. His hands landing on top of hers, he enveloped his dick with her chest and fucked her tits.

With every retreat after a thrust forward, she licked and sucked whatever part of him her mouth could reach until he unloaded on her chest.

"Fuuuuuck." He held the last plunge forward as his cock twitched against her overheated flesh. When he was spent, he bent at the waist, resting on the mattress next to her. Her head and his legs were still hanging off the edge of the bed.

Lazily, Prowler kissed the side of her hip before scooting up on the bed so only his toes hung off. "Come." Using her feet planted against the mattress, she spun around so they were now lying in the same direction.

Prowler was in a post-coital-induced state. He looked blissed out lying face down, with his cheek smashed into the mattress. She turned to face him, so they were mere inches apart and just drank him in. From his full lips to the close-cropped beard that felt like heaven on her skin. His sun-bronzed skin and laugh lines spoke of his hardworking but fun nature.

Once she'd creeped on him enough, she reached for the sheet, but Prowler's growl stopped her. Without opening his eyes, he reached for her breasts and torso, rubbing his cum into her skin. He rubbed and massaged until it was no longer slick. Eventually his hand slowed, then stilled.

"Love your mouth. Love your tits. Love—" Mumbling a list of her most beloved body parts against her skin was a slight stab to her heart.

He didn't know that, and it wasn't his fault,

but she still didn't want to hear it, so she interrupted him.

"Why do you always do that?"

"Do what?"

"Rub your cum into my skin like that?" He did it anytime it wasn't trapped in a condom. If it landed on her skin, he'd rub it until it was gone.

Every single time.

"I want others to smell it, to know you're mine." He confessed sleepily before snoring softly.

That made zero sense, but something did scratch at the back of her brain. However, it was lost as she drifted off to join him.

5

PROWLER

Enjoying some of the best sleep he'd had in years, Prowler was a little disturbed when he was pulled to wakefulness by soft curses.

Rubbing the fogginess from his eyes, he rolled over and searched the mostly dark room for the source.

Taylor.

She was crawling around the floor, face down, looking under the dresser. Ass all the way up in the air. Obviously searching for her clothes that had been carelessly tossed away last night.

She looked downright edible like that. Like she was begging to be taken from behind while he fisted her hair or, better yet, held her down with his mouth to her neck.

Where the hell did that come from?

As soon as he thought it, he knew the wolf smiled. The rumble the beast emitted, he could damn near feel it deep in his chest.

Prowler had always felt as if they were separate entities, disconnected, but stuck together because he was the only option at the time.

The quantum wolves he knew felt the same, so it was assumed that was just the way it was for them. However, the way it felt right then had him questioning that.

For the first time since their circumstances brought them together, they were in harmony, like two halves that were trying to come together.

When the next words left his mouth, they came out rough and wild.

"I wanna bite that ass hard enough to leave a mark." He growled, or rather his wolf did.

Another first.

Taylor startled and turned in his direction. Her green eyes looked surprised in the low light.

Interesting, he made a mental note to mention that to Kansas, but when she stood and turned her entire body his way, his world narrowed down to her.

"Not going to happen. We start that, and I'll forget my own name."

He chuckled. "That's kind of the point, sweetheart." Prowler patted the space beside him on the mattress. "Come back to bed."

He heard the difference or rather felt it. It wasn't just for round four, he wanted her there. In his bed, his home, his life. To hell with doubts and questions. They could figure it out together. After last night, the dinner, the effort she put into Cass, into him, it was clear their no-strings arrangement had grown friggin' ropes, and he wasn't mad about it.

Taylor, however, would be. She was as no-strings as he had been.

"If I come over there, you'll pull me down to the bed and fuck me stupid. I can't let that happen. We need to talk."

Taylor spoke as she pulled her shirt over her head, forgoing the bra. Maybe that's what she'd been looking for under the dresser.

"The dreaded four words no man wants to hear," Prowler quipped as he turned on the bedside light and scooched up so he was reclined against the headboard, not bothering with covers.

"It's about our arrangement." She crossed her

arms under her chest, leaning back against the dresser after pulling on her leggings.

Hope flared in his chest. Maybe she wanted more too.

With a smile, he reached down and gripped his shaft. Loving the way her eyes followed his movement, he slowly stroked up and down. The appreciation and longing in her gaze were all the boost he needed.

"What a coincidence. I was thinking the same thing."

Her eyes left his cock and clashed with his.

The look in her peridot gaze most certainly didn't mirror his own. Hers was more on the sad and disappointed side rather than hopeful and happy.

Shit, he fucked up. She must've thought he was ending things.

"Taylor, I—"

She cut him off.

"Please can I go first?"

"No."

He knew what her response would be. It was the same anytime someone told her no; she acted like she didn't comprehend the word.

"No?"

And he knew what his response would be ... the same as it was any time she used no as a question.

"Yeah, no." Prowler stood and stalked over to her. Invading her space so she had no retreat. "Because." He pulled one of her crossed arms down and placed it on his shoulder.

"If you go first." He repeated the motion with the other. "You're going to give me some it's not you, it's me speech." He placed his hands under her luscious ass and lifted. "And walk out the door."

Turning with her in his arms, he laid her on the bed, coming down half on top of her, pinning her down with his leg. Looking deep into the eyes he lov... no, really, *really* fucking liked ... a lot.

He was experiencing weird intermittent emotions, like a radio station fading in and out, but they didn't feel like they were solely his. His were certainly going haywire too, but to have other bursts coming through was disturbing. He realized it was the wolf. He was feeling the wolf's feelings sporadically.

"And that wouldn't give me a chance to say that I want to renegotiate our agreement."

"First off, I wasn't going to say it was me and

not you because it was totally you, buddy. And second, what do you mean renegotiate? Isn't that what I was going to do?"

"No."

"No?"

There it was again. He never realized how endearing it was before.

"Yeah, no. You were about to terminate, not negotiate." He nipped her lip. "And what do you mean it's me? I'm a fucking delight, and you said so yourself. I can fuck you stupid. What more could you ask for in your man?" He flashed her his most predatory smile, and Wolf approved.

Something about the new connection with his wolf had him thinking of him as Wolf, not just a wolf.

"My man, huh?" He could see the skepticism in her captivating eyes. "I thought we agreed no strings. When it's over, it's over, and we remain neighbors and friends. *My man* sounds pretty stringy to me."

Taylor tried to worm her way out from under him, but he didn't allow it.

"Hence my use of renegotiate. But we'll circle back to that. What do you mean it's totally me?" Something about the hurt that flashed across her face when she'd said that had his hackles raised.

"You." She stopped abruptly and tried to wiggle free again.

What the fuck?

As a rule, Taylor was putty in his hands when he turned up the charm, but she really wasn't falling for his seduction. Things were going south, and fast.

"Please, Prowler, let me go. I need to think straight, and I can't do that like this."

What had she seen or found out about him that had her needing to think straight to kick him to the curb?

A million thoughts flew at him at once, but he shifted his body weight enough for her to move.

Did she know about the less-than-legal businesses he was involved in? The girls, the books, the gambling? How they collected when someone welched? How they dealt with threats to the club or their secrets?

Could she feel the blood on his hands when he touched her? Looking down at the hands in question, he almost expected to see crimson.

Then, an even more terrifying thought chilled him to the bone.

Did she know about Wolf?

Wolf bristled at the thought.

The only reason their kind held their secret as long as they had was because the only people who knew were either dead or family. That was the first thing Kansas ever taught him about having a fur side. Dead or family, and family was bound together by blood, and not the kind flowing through their own veins.

First and foremost was protecting that information. The general population didn't know they existed. A shudder wobbled down his spine. There wasn't a doubt in his mind that if their secret got out, they'd be locked away and experimented on by the government, much like Domino pack had done to their own but on a much larger scale, if not just out and out eliminated due to fear, that is.

Prowler stood, grabbing his jeans. Pulling them on, he didn't bother to button them.

He didn't like the turn things had taken.

He felt vulnerable, a sensation he hadn't experienced in a really long time.

Anger at the situation flooded him. He was finally ready to settle down, give a relationship a go, and the universe instead just brandished the giant dildo of not a fucking chance, sans lube.

Prowler stared at her as she chewed her lip. He couldn't kill her, wouldn't. Fuck the rules. He could force her to be family, but he couldn't trust that. The only solution was to lock her away until she developed Stockholm syndrome or some shit.

But fuck him sideways, he couldn't do that either.

While he was lost in thought, Taylor started speaking. Instead of hearing her words, he just watched her mouth move.

When he finally tuned back in, she was trying to brush past him.

"Your silence speaks loud and clear, Prowler."

"Wait." He caught her in his arms, but she stayed stiff.

"Why wait? So we can drag this out? You broke our agreement, and then you tried to renegotiate it. Why? To hurt me? Mission accomplished."

He'd never heard her sound so defeated, and it damn near broke him. Wait, what did she say?

Relief and confusion warred within him. Relief his furry secret was still safe, and confusion because what the hell had she just said that he confirmed with silence?

"What are you talking about? I didn't break

shit, Taylor. I haven't touched another woman. Not just since we've been fucking but even before. Since the first time I saw you, really saw you, and you fucking yelled at me about my trash cans." He hadn't meant to confess that, but he also hadn't meant to let his anger control him, but there they were. His temper rising.

"Wow. It took you a long time to come up with that diversion." She took a deep breath. "It's better this way, really. I'm not relationship material on the best of days, and neither are you. But let's face it, a steady hook-up is a relationship no matter how you slice it. That's not what either of us wanted or needed."

Prowler didn't miss the slight upward inflection she ended with. Turning her statement into more of a question. He also didn't miss the past tense. Could that mean she wants and needs it now?

She had doubts, and he could exploit that.

"Babe. We're going to be dizzy with all the circling back we'll have to do, but first, I want you to repeat whatever it was you said that you think I did."

"Your ex."

"My ex? What about her?"

"You're together again or whatever it is. I get it, there's history. That's hard to let go of sometimes. So just let me bow out gracefully and keep some of my dignity intact. Especially where Cass is concerned."

He'd be lying if he said the fact she was thinking about his daughter and her feelings, even when she was clearly going through her own, didn't give her a bit more real estate in his heart. But he had to put a stop to her worry where Allie was concerned.

Gripping her cheeks in his hands, forcing eye contact. "You hear me right fucking now. Allie is nothing more than the woman who gave birth to my daughter. There is not, and never will be, anything between us."

Instead of hope flaring in her eyes, the green reflected hurt and anger.

"I never thought you'd lie to me, Prowler. I knew when I met you that I'd end up in too deep, and you'd break a part of my soul, but I never thought it would be because of a lie."

Wow, she sounded disappointed in him, and that almost stung worse than all the other shit—almost.

"I'm not fucking lying, Tay. There's nothing going on."

"Gah." She pulled away from him. "Quit lying. I saw it myself. You locked lips with her right out there for anyone to see." She waved toward the front of the house as a tear fell from her shimmering eyes.

Wolf stood at attention in the front of his mind. Head cocked to the side, listening and growling. It was the first time he was in the driver's seat when in skin, and it felt strange ... but kinda right.

"You won't even kiss me in private, but you had no shame about locking lips with her on the front porch in front of half of your club."

She dashed away tears.

Wolf paced and turned his anger on Prowler.

Fix this. Those two words floated through his mind.

"Did you know I stole a kiss tonight while you slept? I needed to know what your lips felt like on mine before I ended things. How pathetic is that?"

Wolf howled long and loud. Calling to Taylor. Prowler didn't know how he knew that's what it was, but he did.

She dashed more tears from her cheeks.

"And now I'm crying, and I hate to fucking cry. You have no idea of the shit I've gone through. Unwanted touches from those I should've been able to trust. Fucking beatings and broken bones. I endured it all without so much as a whimper. Now I'm crying over a man I tried so hard not to fall for but failed. I let you make me weak, Prowler, and I may never forgive you for that. I fought so hard to be strong, and I gave that up for mind-blowing sex, and I'll never forgive myself for that."

Taylor stormed out before he could think straight. The sound of the front door lock engaging told him she'd left his house.

Moments later, everything she'd confessed became clear. Prowler was blown back with a typhoon of swirling emotions.

He was trying to sift through them as he got dressed to go show Taylor exactly what the new terms of the arrangement were.

Anger, Wolf's and his, had his eyes flickering back and forth, a change threatening.

"Calm down, Wolf, we'll fix it."

I want their blood.

He was fully on board with Wolf wanting

blood from whoever had silenced her tears in the past.

"Hey, you spoke directly to me?" Prowler mused aloud as he donned a shirt.

Well, you finally spoke directly to me, asshole.

Prowler hadn't realized it until Wolf said it. In the last thirteen years, Prowler just kinda thought things, and Wolf either went along with it or pushed against it.

He had never taken the time to speak to him.

"You're not exactly Mr. Congeniality yourself, fuzzy butt."

Wolf growled, but it was a different kind of rumble. Prowler was realizing that Wolf had been communicating with him all along, just not with words. Wolf had a full vocabulary of sounds.

Maybe not all quantums had to have such a dysfunctional relationship with their animals. If that was the case, this new information could change the lives of some of his brothers for the better.

There was a burning question Prowler had based on what Kansas and Hunter had mentioned about Naturals.

"Do you see things ... I mean, through my eyes ... that I don't?"

Sometimes.

"Did you see Taylor kiss me?"

Kiss us, yes.

"Did you feel it?" He wasn't sure why he was asking, but he needed to know. He was terrified and exhilarated at the same time. He wanted something from their first kiss. Since he was asleep, he was hoping that ...

In a manner of speaking, yes.

"Is—"

Enough questions. I have one for you.

Instead of speaking aloud, he did a mental answer to get the feel of conversing with Wolf quietly too.

Are you going to stay here like a pussy, or are we going after her?

Prowler laughed, actually laughed. And the chuffing sound from Wolf was basically lupine laughter.

We just shared a laugh. Prowler sent silently to Wolf.

Wow, a decade and a half. That's a hell of a learning curve you've got, slugger.

The slugger comment brought him up short. Wolf was telling him without telling him that he saw a lot through his eyes.

Locking the door behind him, he mentally spoke to Wolf as he jogged across the street.

Do you have memories of before?

Before what? Wolf sounded genuinely confused.

Before me.

Some, why? He sounded cautious.

Memories of the ... the man before me?

Why he was asking, he didn't know. Maybe morbid curiosity or maybe to know Wolf better. Or possibly because he still needed to know if it was really a one-off as Allie had said it was.

Her cheating had really fucked with him, and still was. It somehow broke the trust mechanism he had.

Most of my memories are of the times I am running free. The smells, the feel of the earth under my paws, the intensity of it all. Companion memories are ... different. They fade with time. Even while they're happening, they are dull, hazy, except ...

Wolf trailed off as they approached Taylor's house, and the sounds of heavy music and growling vocals were pulsing from the far side.

Following the sound, Prowler found her garage door about a third of the way up with light and sound spilling out. As he ducked under, he never expected the sight before him.

Taylor was beating and kicking the shit out of a heavy bag in nothing but a tee shirt, underwear, and taped hands. She was sexy as fuck.

And she was damn good.

Wolf chuffed his approval. He recognized the sound as pride.

I second that.

He was so turned on that the zipper was biting into his dick until her voice cut through a lower part of the song.

She was chanting insults at herself every time she connected with the bag. When he heard, "I deserved it. I always deserved it." Prowler was propelled into action.

Closing the distance between them, he scooped her up from behind. She screamed and began punching behind her. He took the abuse.

"Babe, it's me. It's me." After a while, she stopped fighting back.

"Prowler?" He heard the tears before he saw the evidence—the red glistening eyes, the trails down her cheeks.

"Yeah, babe."

When he felt her body relax, he lowered her

until she stood on the floor. Turning her to face him, he cupped her cheeks.

"You deserved none of the bad shit ever done to you. And one day, I will have names. The only thing you deserve is love, Taylor. Love and security." He dropped a kiss on her forehead. "And I plan on being the man to give it to you."

Taylor stared at him for so long he thought she'd never speak again.

When her smile finally came, it wasn't the beaming one he expected when she was overjoyed. No, it was a cautious one. Like she didn't trust herself to hope or trust Prowler's words.

"How can you say that? We've fucked around for a few months, but you don't know anything about me. Hell, I don't know anything about you either. Like your favorite color or—"

"Jade."

"What?"

"My favorite color. Jade, like your eyes."

Eyes that promptly rolled at his words. "My point is, we don't know each other. I don't even know your first name."

"I know if I kiss you here." Prowler nipped the area where her shoulder met her neck. He tasted the saltiness on her skin from her earlier exertion.

But underneath that was her intoxicating scent of sweet coffee and musk. "Your knees buckle." As if on cue, he grabbed her hips as her legs wobbled.

"That's irr—"

"Riley. Riley Reynolds." He didn't need to add the last name. She knew that from the school pick-up slip she signed that was Cassady's last name.

"You're just making my point for me." Her voice came out husky and breathless, and he wanted nothing more than to pound into her body like a madman. He knew that would be a mistake and validate her doubts.

"We've never even been on a date. No movie, no dinner. Nothing but sex. I know from experience that sex is nothing to build a relationship on. I've got the emotional trauma and restraining orders to prove it. And it wasn't even that good."

Prowler let her go and turned as quickly as preternaturally possible. He didn't want to, but he had to. He felt it coming. Wolf was practically thrashing against him, howling to get out. To kill everyone who came before them.

While he could control the change, he couldn't control the eyes. They always gave him away.

Neither man nor beast would stand for her talking about dick from another man.

"Go answer your front door, Tay." He spoke without turning around while striding toward the garage door.

"What?"

"Just answer the fucking door," he said in a singsong voice to mask his rising anger and impending change.

While jogging around the house, he talked Wolf down. When they found the fuckers she mentioned, the abusive one, the one she mentioned in the garage, and anyone else who hurt her, he promised Wolf a kill.

By the time he was ringing her front bell, Wolf was satisfied with their agreement and melted back into the shadows.

The door flew open, and Taylor stood there, still dressed in barely anything, with her arms crossed over her chest.

"What are you playing at, Prowler? I'm tired."

"Riley, and I wanted to know if you'd like to go to dinner and a concert with me Friday? There's a great local metal band playing on Fremont, and the pizza place close by has great pie. Even vegan if you want."

Prowler watched, amused as she tried to fight the smile that was tugging at her luscious lips. Lips he needed to taste. He was jealous that Wolf knew them, and he didn't.

Prowler could tell it was a yes before she spoke because of her eyes. They were so expressive and conveyed her every emotion. Which is probably why he avoided looking into them when the sex was really good. He would've given in and kissed her if he had.

Why not now, though?

What if she wasn't the one? The question bounced around his brain. They were starting something, and even if she wasn't, he'd never kiss another to find out. But then he remembered the wondering.

Could he spend a lifetime wondering? Wolf didn't seem to share his doubts.

"Okay, Riley. You had me at metal. I'll go out with you."

His name on her lips was like a song from a choir. It moved him in unexpected ways.

"Perfect. I'll pick you up at seven. Wear boots and sleeves." She was going to be on the back of his fucking bike, and she was going to be his.

Prowler couldn't hide the shit-eating grin that took over his face.

Fuck wondering.

Grabbing her cheeks and pulling her lips to his, he kissed her hard. She didn't open to him, but he didn't expect her to. He knew it would shock her too much to respond.

The tingling that ran from his lips, through his bloodstream, and culminated in an explosion in his chest was new and telling. If that hadn't been enough, Wolf's howl was.

She is mine, he thought with wonder.

Ours, Wolf corrected.

Turning, he jogged back across the street, stopping halfway across her yard when he realized two things.

One, the sliver of light from her house was still streaming across the desert landscaping, and two, she didn't ask about Allie.

Turning, he shouted to grab her attention.

"Taylor." When she looked up at him, he continued. "For the record, I didn't kiss Allie. She kissed me, and I stood there dumbfounded by the unexpected contact, kinda like you are right now. Except I wasn't savoring it. And Taylor?"

He spoke her name again because her eyes had glossed over as her fingers gently caressed her lip.

"Close and lock the door behind you, babe. I'm not leaving until you do."

Prowler waited until he heard the lock engage before jogging back home.

First thing he did after locking his front door was grab a beer and head out back for a smoke. After lighting up, he sat there flicking the top of his lighter rhythmically and thinking about Taylor and the new sensations coursing through his body.

He had so many questions for Wolf and new information to share with his brothers about their state of existence. So much was wrong about what they thought they knew, and so much was right. It was a little overwhelming.

He sat there for close to an hour, just enjoying Wolf's presence for once and mulling over things.

The patio door opened behind him.

"What are you doing awake, Jellybean?"

His daughter took the seat next to him in the Adirondack chair. "I wanted to talk to you about something."

"You can talk to me about anything, you know

that." He turned her way to stub his cigarette out, and she gasped.

Looking into his daughter's face, he saw wonder in her eyes, eyes so much like his own. It reminded him of the way she looked at him as a toddler, like he'd hung the moon.

"Your eyes. I was right, you are a shifter." Before the *oh shit* registered in his thoughts, she had launched herself at him.

6

TAYLOR

Taylor's shift was dragging. It was only four hours long, but it felt like ten. Not that the casino wasn't insanely busy, but because she had a date tonight that she couldn't stop thinking about.

She'd traded her night shift for Theresa's day. When her coworker had jumped at the chance, it raised Taylor's suspicion. She'd thought for sure she'd have to add some sort of incentive, but nope.

Now four ass grabs, two threats of *stop looking at my man, you whore*, and no less than seven interactions with security, Taylor realized the early shift was fucking bedlam.

Changing into running shoes from heels after her shift was one of the little things in life that was underappreciated, she thought as she laced hers up.

"So, Taylor, are you thinking of making the permanent change to days ... coming over to the dark in the light side?"

Claire, the fifty-four-year-old who didn't look a day over forty, asked. Claire had been the one to train her on nights when she'd first got hired. "We have cookies, and better tips."

Taylor couldn't deny the truth of it. She'd made nearly double what she did for a two-hour longer shift at night. However, she'd take the too drunk *Vegas can't handle us* dude bro types over the sobering six a.m. crowd who had a flight to catch so they were shooting their last shot, any day.

"Not a chance in hell, Claire. You can keep your cookies and bruised ass cheeks," she quipped as she closed her locker.

"Your loss," Claire retorted and followed her from the locker room. "I'm set to retire in three months. So, my ass cheeks can recover just fine while I'm floating around in my pool, sipping margaritas all day, and making questionable content in my old age." Claire laughed.

"You ladies ready?" Will asked. Taylor was

grateful that it was the casino's policy to walk the ladies to their car after shift.

Taylor waited with Will for Claire to get into her car and lock the doors before they started toward hers. "I got it from here, Will. Thanks."

"You sure?"

"Yeah. I can see it from here." She pointed proudly at her pride and joy. Just the back quarter panel was visible on the other side of a huge SUV parked beside her. She hoped like hell they hadn't dinged her car with their monster doors.

"That's one sweet ride," Will remarked. Even without much to go on, there was no mistaking the marvel of a classic American muscle car.

"I know." She beamed as she strode toward her car.

"I'll tap the brakes after I'm locked in, and you can head back," she shouted behind her.

"Okay."

Once she was close, she hit the key fob, starting and unlocking the car.

Rounding the SUV, she reached for her door only to realize it was partially open. Her brother sat in the driver's seat.

"Hello, sis," Travis said as he stood from the seat, opening the door all the way. The action herded her toward the front of the car, away from where she could pop out to see Will waiting for the signal.

Travis must've followed her line of thinking because he reached over the top of the open door and loosely grabbed her arm. "I tapped the brakes for you, so your shadow is gone. Besides." His tone turned artificially sweet. "You're safe with me; I'm your brother after all."

"You're no brother to me, Travis. And I told you I was done. Not to come around anymore."

"Technically, you told me not to come to your house, so ..." He trailed off as he shifted his body so he could close the door.

He walked them back in an attempt to trap her, but she stopped her backward retreat.

"Anyway, I need your help."

Taylor was so over it with Travis and men like him in her life.

She.

Was.

Done.

"No more help. I told you. Forget you even know me, Travis. Don't come to my work, my home, hell, don't run into me in public. You see me on the street, turn and walk the other way."

"Not going to happen. We're family, and family is forever, Taylor. Like it or not, that's facts."

"Family? FAMILY?" She yanked her arm from his grasp. "That's rich coming from you. Family doesn't treat each other the way you and Dad treated me. So no, we are not family. I choose my family now, and you are not among them."

"Like that biker trash you're fucking? The one with a hot piece of ass daughter? They're who I need help with actually, so it's perfect that you've sunk so low."

Taylor didn't hear anything but noise after he called Prowler trash and made a comment about Cass that turned her stomach.

"Leave now, Travis, or I'll make you." She spoke with a calm, steady voice.

"You." He laughed as he stroked her cheek. "You'd never hurt me, sweetheart." When his hand started to trail down her neck, she didn't think, just reacted.

Grabbing the offending appendage, she bent it back until Travis screamed and went to the ground. But she didn't stop there. After driving the heel of her other hand into his nose, she raised her foot and planted it hard against his chest until he ended up flat on the concrete.

"DON'T EVER TOUCH ME AGAIN."

Everything started to blur. Taylor had finally fought back, and she felt ... amazing. Adrenaline shakes aside, there was an exhilaration to finally fighting back. She had been training for a day like this since she ran from Billy, but she never thought she'd have to guts to actually fight back. Not to mention, she thought it would be Billy, not Travis, but still.

When he'd touched her, she was right back in her childhood home around the time her dad stopped coming to her room, and Travis started. She'd known then it was only a matter of time before one or both raped her, so she ran.

Then she found herself in a toxic pattern. Going from one abusive relationship to the next. Each time, she ran. Never fighting back, never standing up for herself, just getting the hell out of Dodge. But Taylor was done running. She was fighting back from now on.

It barely registered that another man was lifting Travis up by his armpits and loading him into the SUV beside her.

"Fuck." Travis shook off the assistance as he

stepped up into the SUV. "Took you long enough," he yelled at the other man before turning to her through the open window.

"You fucked up, Taylor. Remember, you left me no choice. I just needed a little help, and everything would've been fine, but now, you've forced my hand."

When she met his eyes, the look on his face was blank. Emotionless. It was disturbing. More so than when he looked at her with lust. With a bloody nose and a sprained wrist at best, his features should've been twisted in agony or something, but they weren't. He was simply there. It was creepy, no emotion at all.

"Enjoy your life while you can, *sister*." Even the words he meant as a parting shot were monotone. She couldn't decide whether that made them more threatening or less.

In a daze, Taylor got in her car and headed home.

She didn't remember much of the drive. Thank God she didn't get into an accident. Donning a sports bra and shorts, she headed to her garage.

It wasn't his threat that occupied her mind or even the flat tone he delivered it in. It was the fact she'd stood up for herself that did it.

An overwhelming sense of power pushed all other thoughts to the background. She wailed on the heavy bag for well over an hour before deciding to run a few miles. She still had some adrenaline to burn off.

She'd stood up for herself.

Ear buds in place and Carcass blasting in her ears, she set a punishing pace. She opted to exit their neighborhood gate to change the scenery a little. Around the back side of the neighborhood, just on the other side of the wall behind her house, she noticed an old beater parked along the road. She had to run past it on the sidewalk anyway, so she slowed her pace to have a look inside. As soon as she came alongside the back bumper, they peeled out, spraying road debris on her legs.

"Rude much?" she shouted toward the taillights.

Finishing up her run, she headed back through the gate, which now hung open. *Ugh.*

She walked up to the keypad and started punching numbers like that would fix the damned thing, or something. It was perpetually broken. The HOA had replaced it twice in the last year, and yet it was still only secured fifty percent of the time. Of course, they still collected one hundred percent of their dues each month. The only thing their two hundred bucks a month went to was landscaping, the five private roads in the community, and the damn gate.

You'd think they could do better. "Maybe I should run for president and make the damn gate a priority." She muttered to herself as she entered her neighborhood.

The events of the morning and lazy HOAs aside, she was determined to enjoy tonight.

Prowler wasn't the dating type, but he was making an effort, so she'd be damned if her brother would spoil the night for her.

Her makeup for the night was a breeze. Skipping the foundation, she opted for heavy eyeliner and mascara, with a red lip.

She donned a red lace thong and push-up bra that Prowler had yet to see before rummaging through her closet.

"There you are. Come to mama." She pulled out her favorite ripped jeans. The pair that every girl has for date night that makes her ass look amazing. Yeah, those.

She paired it with a sliced-up Exmortus tee from the last time she saw them live and her concert boots. They were black and covered in chains and buckles, plus a silver CU dangling down the back of the left one and NT hanging down the back of the right one.

Looking at herself in the mirror, she felt beautiful. "One finishing touch." She told her reflection, reaching for her battle vest, until she remembered they were riding to the show, and she needed sleeves. Trading the denim vest for a long-sleeved, faux leather jacket.

No sooner had she pushed her arms through the sleeves than her doorbell rang.

Opening it without checking the peephole, she found a sexier than sin Prowler looking every inch a predator. A yummy, ferocious, blond-haired Viking-looking predator ready to pillage and plunder—

"Wow." He interrupted her naughty thoughts. "I was ready to paddle your ass raw for just flinging the door open without checking who it was, but damn, mama, you stole the words right out of my mouth."

Prowler stepped just inside the door, widening his stance and wrapping his arms around her waist. He nibbled her neck and ear as always. While it still stung her that his initial greeting wasn't a kiss, she had to admit, she loved their special way too. Besides, he'd kissed her last night, and that had to count for something.

"How do you know I just flung it open?" she challenged breathlessly.

"Because." Nip. "No shadow." Suck.

"Maybe I checked my app and saw it was you."

Prowler pulled back with narrowed eyes. She was a shit liar, and she knew it. The truth was always right there on the surface.

"So, where's your phone then?"

"Um." Searching her pockets, she knew she wouldn't find it and, from the look on his face, so did he. "Right ..."

"Right not fucking here." His words were harsh, but his tone was concerned. She couldn't meet his gaze. With the curled knuckle of his index finger, he lifted her chin. "Babe, promise me this is a one-off. You'll check every time from now on."

His concern was so genuine. The look in his eyes almost pulled three words from her lips she was not ready to say, so instead she opted for two. "I promise."

"Good girl." He did a hit-and-run style kiss. An

all too brief meeting of the lips that left her kissing air when he pulled back.

"Now, go find your phone, and let's get going." He swatted her ass as she turned toward her room. This more playful side of Prowler was surprising but not unwelcome. She'd caught glimpses of it before with Cass, but now he seemed more relaxed with her ... with them.

His lips.

It was twice now she'd felt his lips on hers, but it was nowhere near enough. She craved more. More of the sexy man she'd left standing in her living room in all his bad-boy hotness.

When she finally found her phone, she returned to catch him dragging his finger across the spines of her books, which she'd arranged by spice level on her bookshelf, but he didn't need to know that.

She was taking inventory of how yummy he looked—from the faded black jeans that cupped his ass just right, to the way his biceps pushed the thread holding the seams of his black Henley together to its limits.

Her gaze traveled up his back, past the bottom rocker that read NEVADA, over the crowned skull wearing a bandana, and the lettering above it proclaiming him a King, to the messy bun gathered low.

The little peeks of his neck she glimpsed through the strands escaping were sexier than she ever would've imagined. She hated man-buns with a passion, or so she thought.

"Boy, was I wrong," she breathed out.

Taylor hadn't realized she'd spoken aloud until his finger stopped and traveled to the top of the book he was touching as he spoke.

"Wrong about what?" He asked without turning away from the shelf, while at the same time tipping the book out of the row and leaning over to see the now half-exposed cover.

Her gaze laser-focused in on the book he had tipped out and was now holding in his hands. Fuck. Why it bothered her, she didn't know. She wasn't ashamed of her reading choices, never was and never would be. She was an unapologetic smut slut. But something about him touching *His Lost Mate* by Theresa Hissong caused goose bumps to break out all over her skin.

As he caressed the cover and flipped it over, he might as well be doing the same to her body because she was feeling the ghost of his touch as he dragged his hand along the cover and inserted a finger between the pages before opening it wide.

Head tilted toward the pages but looking at her, he grinned. A big bad wolf about to eat the little girl in the red cloak kind of grin. That fucker knew. Knew what he was doing to her.

"So, you like it dirty, do you?"

Fuck that noise. The man had fucked her in almost every way one could fuck another. She wouldn't play the virgin now.

Meeting his gaze unwaveringly, she answered. "You know I do."

"But this." He closed the book, taking a step toward her while holding the cover out for her to see. "You like the thought of a shifter in your bed? Doing all those things to your body while a wolf simmers just below the surface." He took another step, and she felt like a small prey animal. "Waiting to pounce. To bite you. To mark you as his forever."

Taylor's breath hitched. Cass's suspicions raced to the front of her mind. If this was the Prowler Cass had meant, Taylor could see it one hundred and ten percent. If shifters were real, then yes, Prowler would definitely be one.

He was upon her before she breathed again.

Tossing the book onto the table behind her, he caged her in against it. Prowler dropped his mouth to her ear. "Does the thought of a man losing control to his inner beast while fucking you senseless turn you on? Holding you in place with his teeth so you can't move while he claims you?"

His question was a growl that vibrated down to her clit.

"Yes. Fuck yes," she answered in all honesty. If it weren't so appealing, there wouldn't be thousands of best-selling romance novels about it.

One arm of her cage disappeared, and she felt a hand unzipping her jeans.

"Fuck," he cursed when he couldn't wedge his hand down the front of her too-tight pants. The jeans were designed to make her ass look good, not for quick access.

Prowler pulled away enough to work her jeans just below her hips, granting him access with his hand and nothing more.

Dipping his mouth back to her neck, his fingers dove inside her. "Babe, you're so wet for me. I think my beauty really does want a beast in her bed."

His finger glided toward her back entrance. Before she could protest, it was gone, traveling toward her clit and gathering moisture along the way. He started with an up and down motion that switched to tight rapid circles just when she needed it. There was no denying the man was a fucking expert in that department. He worked her clit like a professional with a doctorate in clitology.

A master clitologist if you will.

"Fuck, Riley. I'm coming."

"Hell, yeah, you are. Come on my hand, babe, and scream my name to the night."

"Riley." She drew out the last syllable before her legs gave out. Prowler held her close until she could stand again.

"That was beautiful," he praised her as he sucked his fingers. "Absolutely stunning."

Taylor couldn't look away as she righted her jeans.

"You wanna taste the sweetest ambrosia, Taylor?" He asked while extending his hand toward her mouth. Still buttoning her jeans, she dipped her face forward to suck his offered fingers into her mouth, but before she could wrap her lips around them, he said, "I have a better idea."

Then he did it.

He kissed her.

And not the mere meeting of lips from before, no, this time he devoured her mouth. A real kiss.

Taylor's hands were trapped between them as he held her in place for his oral assault. That's what it was too. He was laying siege to her mouth.

And boy could he kiss! His tongue explored every inch of her mouth. Every so often, he pulled back just enough to suck her bottom lip between his.

After what felt like hours, she realized she wasn't an active participant in the kiss she'd been longing for, dreaming of.

Fuck that.

She ripped her hands from between them, not caring if her jeans were buttoned or not, and buried her fingers in that messy bun.

Prowler growled.

A rumble she felt in her bones.

When their lips finally parted, they were both left panting.

"You're mine, Taylor," he growled in a voice that didn't seem to belong to him. "Do you hear me? You're mine."

Too dumbfounded to speak, she nodded. Prowler felt different somehow. Everything about him seemed, well, different is the only word to come to mind. His voice, his posture, his ... eyes. Yes, even his eyes—the way he looked at her was new.

Taylor marked it down to the kiss and the date creating a giddy atmosphere. Their relationship was changing, so of course she'd see it through a different lens. She kept pushing the doubts down. She wanted to believe his declaration without hesitation. It wasn't easy, not with her history, but she would try.

With an extra spring in her step, she headed for the door. "Hurry up, I don't want to miss the opening band. You're going to love Radio Cowboy."

Once outside, Prowler handed her a helmet as he waved across the street. "Keep your eyes open, Kansas."

Following his line of sight, she could barely make out one of his brothers in the shadows by the front of his house. Prowler must have better than 20/20 vision to see that far.

Or he's a wolf, and shifters are real.

That was another thing she pushed aside, trying to puzzle out the mystery Cass planted in her head. Just for the night. There would be time enough for that later.

As she donned her helmet, she faintly heard. "Will do, *Riley*." That was the first time she'd ever heard any of them use his name. It was usually Prez this and Prowler that. Never Riley.

Her suspicions were confirmed when Prowler's response was issued. "You'll pay for that."

"Worth it, Prez. Totally worth it. You kids have fun tonight."

It finally registered in her brain the drawn-out, feminine way he'd said *Riley*.

"Oh my god." She slapped Prowler's shoulder as he mounted the bike in front of her. "He heard me."

Embarrassment shot through her even before Prowler confirmed her suspicion.

"Don't worry, babe. He'll pay for it." He fired up the engine and tapped his helmet, opening the comm since the bike was too loud to shout over. "No one gets to have any of you but me. That includes your cries of pleasure."

So much was wrong with that statement, but at the same time, so much was right with it too.

"How ..." was all she could manage. She'd known she was loud, but that loud? That seemed like quite a stretch even for her vocal range.

"He's a natural with excellent hearing even in sk—from far away."

A natural what? A natural at hearing? That made no sense. And far away had not been what he had started to say. Taylor would bet money on it.

Her mind was turning over the last week, even as she told herself to leave it alone for the night. All the little things that had her questioning, well, everything. From Cass's suspicions about her dad, to Travis coming at her at work the way he did, to Prowler's *you're mine* proclamation.

She was going to have to sit down with a bottle of wine and her thoughts. Get them all together and see what picture the broader strokes made, other than Prowler's a wolf, and Travis was plotting something bad. She was also going to have to call Terry and find out what Travis had on him that caused him to sell her out to the pathetic excuse of a man they shared DNA with.

Prowler parked a block away from the venue, but the music was already pulsing and soothing her soul. Hopping off the bike, she handed her helmet to Prowler and started power walking toward the entrance.

"Come on, they've already started."

"Damn, already so demanding." He looked at his wrist where a watch should be.

"Twenty minutes into being mine," he said with humor, and he caught up to her, wrapping his strong arms around her. He'd pushed up his sleeves and some ink was showing.

"So sexy," she said as she ran her hand along his forearm that was still wrapped around her waist as they approached the security guy.

"Yes, you fucking are." He kissed the side of her head before releasing her and grabbing his wallet.

As soon as the wristband was on, she bolted through the door and up to the rail with Prowler trailing behind.

With horns high, she was in her happy place. Nothing was going to ruin her night.

Taylor turned in his arms between sets and buried her face in his chest inhaling his smoke and pine scent. That smell was now permanently a part of her happy place.

It was well after midnight when they were mounting Prowler's bike to go home.

A windowless creeper van slow-rolled past them before exiting onto the street. It had been parked close by.

Something about it made the hair on the back of her neck stand on end.

She's just donned her helmet and hadn't pulled the visor down yet, but she could've sworn Travis was in the passenger seat glaring at her.

He blocked her view of the driver, but something about the way he gripped the steering wheel had the bottom dropping out of her stomach.

Just when she'd thought this was a perfect night, her paranoia had to creep in.

It had to be that because she refused to accept anything else, dammit. The date—both company and activity—was perfect.

She'd just started to have a life, one like she'd always dreamed of, and she'd be damned if anyone or anything was going to ruin it.

Taylor held on tight to Prowler as they headed back home. His arm resting across her knee with his strong hand stroking her calf erased all the bad from the last week.

She squeezed her eyes tighter and tighter every time a thought other than how great their date was tried to creep into her brain.

7

PROWLER

While it had always been a possibility that Cass would find out, Prowler willfully lied to himself about it, thinking it wouldn't happen yet or that she'd find out after she was married and had kids of her own. Maybe he believed she would remain ignorant forever.

Either way, he'd been wrong. He'd also been wrong about her reaction. She was excited, not horrified. Best of all, she didn't see him as a monster.

Truth be told, that was his biggest fear. That was the number one reason he'd lied to himself about the reality of her finding out. But she allayed all his fears in that department.

That damn kid brought tears to his eyes. It was

his job to do that for her, but she'd turned the fucking tables.

So, there he sat, goofy grin in place as they held an emergency meeting. This time MC and shifter business blended together.

His brothers had yet to ask how she'd found out, assuming he'd told her. It was something they'd discussed when Allie agreed to let her visit more, so of course they assumed that was how it went down. No, they were lost in his happiness as much as he was.

He was loath to break up the mood, but the rest would need to be discussed and with haste.

"I think it's great news, Prez. One less thing to worry about. And ... she's blood." Bulldog was a supportive motherfucker. A hell of a vice and friend, but the last words gave him pause.

She's blood.

Prowler knew beyond a shadow of a doubt that it was spoken with the best of intentions, but it struck a chord. Family and club were blood. Only blood could hold the secret. Shared or shed, it didn't matter, but only blood.

Shared was self-explanatory.

Shed was a little stickier—meaning your own

was shed because, let's face it, dead men don't talk.

Or you shed someone else's as witnessed by the club.

It was a blood-bound secret.

Shared or shed.

Blood in, blood out.

That ripped Prowler out of the warmth his daughter's acceptance had wrapped around him.

"That brings me to how she came about her conclusion."

"Her conclusion?" Kansas asked. "You didn't tell her?"

"She's a smart kid, you know that. Well, apparently, she'd been gathering clues for a while. She thought we were some mafia-esque crime organization." He chuckled a little at the thought. She had the mafia part wrong, but the rest wasn't all that far off the mark.

At least two brothers choked on their drink of choice.

"Fuck, Prez. You didn't tell your teenage daughter about—"

Prowler stood so fast his chair toppled over.

"Get the fuck out. Now." Chef blanched at the

order. Prowler had never kicked a patch out of church before.

"Yes, Prez." He cowered as he exited the sanctuary.

Chef was a mouthy fucker for a human, yet he'd just acquiesced with zero hesitation. That wasn't like him at all.

Prowler scanned his brothers looking for answers to Chef's change of attitude.

The room was eerily quiet. His shifter brothers had their heads tipped back, and his human brothers had their heads bowed. All but Bulldog, who wouldn't make eye contact with him and seemed to be extremely uncomfortable.

"What's going on?" Prowler asked, his voice unsure and questioning.

"Ahem." Bulldog cleared his voice, still not making actual eye contact. "It seems that quantums can be alphas after all."

Prowler felt his brows drop in confusion. When he slumped back into his chair, his brothers seemed to be released from whatever stupor they'd been in.

"Prez, this is ... interesting," Kansas said with excitement directed at Prowler before seemingly talking to himself. "It was only ever a theory, but it is believed that quantums could, under the right set of circumstances, become alpha. But they could never prove ..."

Kansas's one-man conversation came to a halt, and his eyes flew to Prowler. "Did your wolf talk to you?" Without waiting for Prowler's answer, Kansas blurted out. "Did you find your mate?"

Yes. Wolf howled. Prowler mirrored that sentiment.

"Yes and yes. Taylor is my mate and will be my ol' lady." The chatter around him became almost deafening.

All his brothers, even the ones without a furry side, were blown away by the information. Hell, Prowler had been himself when it all started happening, so he understood the excitement.

They had been operating blind, so to speak, for years. The only information they had for sure was what Kansas's old pack had gleaned through unconscionable research and what he'd learned growing up with wolves.

Hunter and Monster were also both naturals. However, Monster was raised by his human mother with other humans, and Hunter's shifter dad passed when he was seventeen, but they'd never been part of a pack.

They'd been winging it for years, and in all those years, there had been zero evidence that quantum had mates or could bond-*bond* with their wolves the way naturals did ... until now.

"This changes so much," Monster breathed out in wonder.

"Does anyone object to me making Taylor my ol' lady? Speak now."

No one spoke, so his brothers banged their fists against the table and whooped. He had his answer.

Prowler hated to drag the mood down, but he had to, so he changed the subject. He would much rather enjoy their happiness and talk about the bond ... both bonds. The need to learn every morsel he could was only overridden by keeping their secret and club business.

"What could possibly be more pressing than the bomb you just dropped?"

"Loose lips."

"Whose?" Bulldog growled. Being the lone bear among wolves and humans had to be difficult. And even though bears didn't run in large packs as wolves did, he knew the importance of keeping a low profile.

"Some kid named Alexander. Senior at Cass's school. He was pivotal in her figuring out about Wolf. Like I said, she'd been collecting evidence, for lack of a better term, for a while. She couldn't puzzle out what I was hiding, although according to her, she would've eventually, with or without his help." He smiled with a bit a pride. His daughter really was too smart for her own good.

"Anyway, when he told her his brother was a wolf by way of his friend's death when they were in a car together, and he mentioned some of his qualities, she said everything just clicked."

"Fuck." That curse came from multiple brothers in the room, all thinking what he was.

"Yeah. Fuck is right."

"How do we contain this, Prez?" Ghoul asked in a monotone. Prowler never doubted his SAA's ability to follow orders, but he could tell he did not relish the thought of silencing an idiot kid just because he and his brother didn't understand the consequences of his condition.

"With blood." Before he could elaborate, Ghoul was out of his chair and ready to shrug off his cut.

"Sit down, not like that. We make them blood. We bring the brother in as a prospect. Teach him what little we fucking know. Alexander follows as soon as he graduates. He can hang around, clean the clubhouse and shit. We'll put him to work, teach him a skill. Then when he's ready, he can prospect too. Blood."

The way Ghoul sagged into his chair rankled a bit. "Did you really think I'd have you eighty-six a kid and a fresh wolf as my first course of action?"

"Deep down? No, Prez, I don't. My brain just went into *protect the secret at all costs* mode. And that was what came to my twisted mind. I just know I'm not man enough to pay that cost."

Agreements rose from everyone in the room. They were all killers, all had blood on their hands, claws, and or teeth, but never like that. Never a woman or a kid.

"Golden and Ghoul, I'll leave the contact up to you. I have all the info I got from Cass on them. The brother is Zachary. Mid to late twenties, works at a dive off the strip."

"Good as done, Prez," Ghoul responded.

"As for Alexander, I told Cass to invite him over for video games and shit. I'll have a chat with him then. Boogeyman, you join us?"

"Sure thing, Prez." Boogeyman was practically vibrating in his chair.

"Your skills will come in handy." For a grown-ass man, Boogey logged way too many hours on video games. Before he joined the Kings, he'd competed ... at video games. Prowler had no idea until he'd met him that gaming was an honest-to-goodness sport.

Every so often, their treasurer would dip out for a week or two for a big competition, but more for fun nowadays.

There was a reason Prowler invited him. If you wanted to win over a teenager, you had to offer up a pretty girl they liked, which Prowler would be fucked all to hell if that would happen. Cass was off-limits to members and horny teens alike.

Or you have to offer up a video game legend. That he had and wasn't opposed to utilizing.

"So, before we stir this shit stew up and take a spoonful, anything else anyone wants to toss in the pot?"

"Sorry, Prez, but the visit with Travis's brother was pretty much a bust. He said he washed his hands of his brother months ago. Didn't know where he was and didn't care to. He had some things to say about old Travi-boy that were less than flattering. I got the impression he was part of the reason why the sister just ..." He made a poof motion.

"Brother said she ran away, and he didn't know where, but I got the impression he might know a bit more. But even with his debt looming out there, I didn't think you'd want us pursuing a traumatized woman who wouldn't piss on her brother if he was on fire."

They were right. They may not follow the law, but they didn't go around hurting women and children either.

"You're right. Well, the money is probably a wash. But it's not the money, it's the reputation of letting it slide that we can do without. Any suggestions?"

"Put the word out that we're willing to offer up his 15K in credit to anyone who puts him in our hands. That sends the direct message that it's not the money, but you don't fuck over the Kings. That will spark the fear of retribution in some and the greed in others. Win-win."

Bulldog was right, and it was a hell of a plan.

"Perfect. Make it so number two," Prowler joked, and the room fell silent again. "What?"

Ghoul burst out laughing. "Prez has got jokes."

He pinged his gaze between a few of his brothers who weren't laughing. "Come on. That shit's funny. It's like Picard."

"We know, jackass. It's just ..." Boogeyman stage whispered. "Prez isn't funny. We're in shock here. Give us a minute."

"What the fuck," Prowler snarled. "I can be funny." When no one agreed, he brushed it aside. "Whatever."

"Any more shit for the stew?"

"No, we want to talk about the bond." This from Golden with Kansas's enthusiastic agreement.

"Adjourned."

Gaveling the meeting closed, they exited for the bar.

After snagging drinks, some members went to shoot pool, while others—the shifters mostly—lingered.

"So, the wolf?" Golden asked. "How?" Of course he was curious, being a quantum himself. He had only lived in the disconnect, as Prowler had done.

"I can't explain it. It was like Kansas always said it was for him. I just talked to Wolf, and he finally answered back."

Kansas sat there just taking it all in while sipping his near beer.

"But why now? What was different?"

Kansas piped in. "Could it be your mate brought him to the surface, so to speak?"

Prowler would love to give Taylor credit, but they had been sleeping together for months. Nothing had ...

"Shit, Kansas, maybe. Taylor kissed me while I was sleeping. I was totally unaware of it, but maybe ..."

Wolf?

What?

Was it her kiss?

Yes and no.

Care to elaborate?

Care to get the fuck out of here and back to our mate?

In due time.

Back atcha.

Prowler felt Wolf retreat back and pace, holding his answers to himself in an attempt to get Prowler to leave.

"Fuzzy Butt is pouting, so I'm sorry, Golden, I don't have any answers."

STOP CALLING ME THAT.

At that, Wolf surged up and took control of his mouth. Sure, Prowler could've halted him but chose not to.

"She kissed the meat bag as he slept. She was leaving us. It was enough to force me to step in because he'd been inside her body for months but refused to recognize her significance."

"Fuck." Prowler wrenched control back and stood. He did not like the control Wolf had. It was wrong, and it made him woozy.

"Whoa, was that ... your wolf speaking?"

Prowler nodded, confused and pissed about what had just happened. They were bound but separate when Wolf chose? It felt wrong, but for all he knew, that was normal. Normal or not, it felt wrong.

"Riley." Kansas spoke in hushed tones. "With a dominant wolf, you have to wrestle him into submission for lack of a better term, or you'll go feral. You two have obviously bound, but as strong as he is, he can surge up and control, well ..." Kansas indicated all of Prowler.

"Which is not exclusively a bad thing, like when the pack—or you—is in danger, for example, but he can't take over like that whenever he wants to."

Kansas looked thoughtful. "It will be a challenge for you, but if anyone is up for it, you are. Shared control like that can be tricky, it's a combination of control and submission."

Prowler let his words sink in.

"Well, I've gotta get home. Cass is coming this week because Allie wants to run off to Cabo to work on her tan or some shit. Let me know if we get a lead on Travis."

"Will do, Prez."

The first thing he did when he got home was grab his laptop and order some groceries. All the vegan shit his daughter loved.

With that mission accomplished, he headed for his back deck and a smoke. After an hour of just relaxing and enjoying the fresh air, he decided to call Taylor.

"Talk to me." She sounded breathless when she answered.

"Hey, beautiful. What are you wearing?"

"Um. A sports bra, shorts, hand tape, and I'm coated in a gallon of sweat."

"Ohhh, sexy."

"You said sexy when you meant gross." Her laugh shot straight to his dick, by way of his heart. Wolf rumbled.

"Can I see you tonight?" He wanted to talk to her. Feel her out. What he hadn't told his club was that Cass had shared her suspicions with Taylor. Taylor wasn't blood yet, and he didn't want to put his brothers in the position of acting or not acting. If shit went south, they'd have plausible deniability.

Once she was his mate or ol' lady or both, blood would protect her.

"That's perfect. There's something I want to talk to you about. I have a thing this afternoon, but after dinner?"

Wolf pricked up.

"I told you I'm in, Tay. You're mine."

"It's not about that. It's more about Cass."

At that, the man perked up too. Was she going to tell him that Cass explained her thoughts to her and gave her the notebook? If she did, he would take that as a very good sign. Borderline acceptance.

"What about her?" He tread lightly, not wanting to really have the meat and potatoes discussion of *I'm a shifter, and you're my one true mate and ol' lady* discussion over the phone.

"Some thoughts she has. About you and your lifestyle. And about this friend Alexander she has."

Both the man and Wolf howled in victory. Prowler didn't plan to say what he did next. Maybe he could blame Wolf for it, but in reality, it was probably all him.

"About me being the big bad wolf?" he teased.

"She told you? I'm so proud of her." *Prowler* was *proud* of Taylor for how she'd encouraged Cass to talk to him.

"It's ridiculous, I know, but she makes a good argument. Sooner or later, you'll have to tell her about your life, or she'll never let the theory go. She'll keep digging until she hits something."

Wolf growled at her dismissal.

"What if it wasn't ridiculous, Taylor? What if her theory was spot on?"

"Well, that ... I mean ... shifters?" Before he could respond, he got a CODE BLACK text.

Fuck.

"Taylor. I gotta go. No time to explain, but tonight might be iffy. I'll call when I can. Love you."

He hung up as soon as the last syllable was out of his mouth. Grabbing his cut off the rack, he headed for the door.

Allie pulled up with Cass just as he was mounting his bike. One of the girls got jumped and on fucking club-owned property. They kept their girls clean and safe, offering their clientele and their girls a top-notch experience. Some fuck-face tainted that, and he'd fucking pay.

"Go inside, sweetheart, and lock the door. I'll be back shortly. Boogeyman will be here in ten. Call Tay to hang out if you want." He kissed Cass's forehead and turned to go, ignoring Allie.

When he said her name, it hit him ... he'd said he loved her. It was true, but he hadn't planned on saying it—any of it actually. He wanted her to fall for him before she knew she held his heart in her tiny, tattooed hands.

"I'll stay until Boogey gets here."

Cass was old enough to stay alone, but Prowler didn't like it. Especially since the indication was that Darcy's beat down was directed at him.

Cass rolled her eyes and headed inside.

Maybe he was being unfair to Allie, and they were finally coming to an understanding. A good place as exes.

"Thanks, Allie."

He was so grateful she volunteered to stay without it being a transaction between the two of them. Perhaps she was turning over a new leaf.

Without thinking, he wrapped his arms around her. When he did, Wolf snarled in disgust and went apeshit. That was overridden because the mother of his child was trembling.

"What's wrong?" he whispered low.

"He's leaving me, and ... and he hit me."

Fuck. When it rains, it pours. He couldn't send his ex or his daughter back to that. However, he couldn't deal with any of it right then. He had to get to the brothel and find out who was using one of the girls to send him a message.

"Go on inside. You can stay in the spare room until I've had a chance to deal with it."

Allie's smile gave him pause. He was just thinking she'd changed, but that smile felt familiar, manipulative and calculating. When his gaze shifted to the car they'd arrived in, his suspicions settled a bit. Gone was the sports car her latest had bought her. She was back in the reliable and sensible mom transport he'd bought.

"Thank you, Riley. I'll be out of your hair tomorrow. The trip to Cabo has turned into a drive to Tucson to check out some places in my parents' neighborhood. Maybe go back to school. Change my stars. Most importantly, stop dating losers."

"You're not taking Cassidy away from me," he

stated rather flatly. Fuck, he was just thinking she'd changed, but the joke was on him.

She pulled a small travel bag from her car. "I know. We have a lot to talk about when you get back. She wants to stay with you, Riley. And with everything going on right now, I think that's for the best."

Other than whatever club shit was going on, things were finally going his way. The smile that split his face could've been spotted from the fucking space station.

Turning, he strode back to Allie and grabbed her bag.

"We'll talk about it when I get back, and I'll help you get a place. Hell, I'll help you with school too."

After setting her bag inside the door, Boogeyman had arrived. That was a relief.

Nodding to his brother, he tossed his leg over his bike and headed out.

She's manipulating you, Wolf stated.

"Are you sure? She seemed sincere to me."

No bitter smell.

"What?"

No fear. If she feared that asshole who hit her, she'd reek of fear, and she didn't.

"Wait, you can smell what I can't when not shifted?"

Now I can, and you can too if you focus, but I'm telling you, Meat Bag, she didn't reek of it. Wolf did not sound pleased.

"If you keep calling me Meat Bag, I get to call you Fuzzy Butt."

Wolf snarled.

Fine.

"Anyway, I saw the bruise on her face when she took off her ridiculously oversized sunglasses."

So he hit her, but she's not scared. Something is up.

"I don't give a shit. She's giving me my daughter, so fear or not, I'm getting that done ASAP."

Hitting his comm button, he called his lawyer, effectively silencing Wolf.

Pulling into the public parking at Royal Arms, Prowler powered off his bike but kept his helmet on to finish the conversation with Langly.

"I'll bring the papers at first light, and you'll be set. I'll file a copy with the courts, but they take the time they take for child support. Could be a month, could be six or more."

"I don't give a rat's ass if the payments cease

or not, so long as Cassidy is legally mine full time."

"Of course. You pay me enough to work all night if needed."

Langly wasn't wrong.

After ending the call, Prowler strode into the hotel they owned, purposefully entering through the legit building first. It was calm as expected. The guests and staff didn't have a clue of the chaos going on just a stone's throw away.

Walking out the back of the hotel, through the courtyard, he came to King's Ransom.

King's Ransom was a club-owned bar with video poker that basically divided the property. Situated directly in front of the private area of the hotel, they familiarly called it the King's Wing.

That building appeared to be old hotel rooms converted to long-term apartments. The brothel was within it, as was their underground casino.

A few of the guys lived in the apartments at the far end. Other rooms served other purposes as needed.

You could only access King's Wing through the back gate, requiring a code, or through an underground tunnel connected to King's Ransom. Since

Prowler wanted to check the state of the hotel guests, he opted for the latter.

Giving Creedence a nod as he strode past the bar, he headed toward the back room and the entrance to the tunnel. Once out of the tunnel, he made a beeline to Darcy's room. Monster was waiting by the door.

"Prez."

"Darcy?"

"Doc just left. Nothing life-threatening, but she'll only talk to you. Doc gave her something for the pain."

"Who was working security?" Prowler's first order of business was to handle the failure in-house before worrying about outside. He already knew the bastard who did this was in the wind.

"The same company we've used for two years when a club member can't be here. Never had a problem until now."

Monster nodded down the hall, and they started walking.

The club was meticulous about security, especially where their less-than-legal businesses were concerned. The company he was referring to wasn't one you could find in the yellow pages. They were underground and paid to be blind to anything not concerning security. They actually contacted Hector through Hunter's cellmate in prison. He was one of Hector's men.

"What did Hector say?"

"He said your call to handle as you see fit. But if he leaves here alive, he won't be for long."

Hector one hundred percent backed the guys he sent to Prowler, but if they fucked up, he washed his hands. Prowler knew he had gang members running security and other odd jobs for him, but they were usually loyal.

"He offered compensation since the failure was his."

Prowler knew that would be Hector's stance, but he wanted to make sure before he did something permanent.

They arrived at one of the rooms that served a special purpose. Using the keypad, they opened the door. It looked like a typical, albeit cramped, long-term stay room. But the smell of blood already had Wolf pacing back and forth.

When they entered the hidden soundproofed room, the smell of blood was overwhelming. The man he assumed was the guard sat tied to a chair, beaten raw. Ghoul was grinning like a loon.

"Kinda looks like a Picasso, huh, Prez?"

"Yeah, kinda." He murmured through his lengthening canines.

Ghoul strode over to the unrecognizable man, yanking his head up by the hair. "You hear that, Matt? My Prez thinks I'm a fucking artist. How cool is that?"

To anyone else, it would appear Ghoul enjoyed his job. That may be a little bit true, but the not so little bit of truth was that he hated people who hurt women more than most, with good reason. Since Matt allowed it, well...

Ghoul watched his mom get beaten, raped, and murdered by rogue shifters. That brought on his first shift, and he destroyed them all, but it fucked him up.

Ghoul shoved the soon-to-be-dead man's head away before punching him again.

"He doesn't want to talk to me, Prez. Guess I'm not his type."

Let me talk to him. Wolf snarled in his head.

Prowler hesitated. This aspect of their relationship was still new, and he wasn't sure about giving up control. When Wolf had taken it earlier, it had exhausted them both.

I'll give it back as soon as he talks. He is keeping us from our mate.

Okay, but no full shifting without my consent.

Kansas had said for a natural, the connection deepens over time, and the two become more like one, and these internal gab sessions won't be the same. They'll just be in sync.

He felt Wolf nod in agreement. *Partial is on the table though*, Wolf added.

Prowler stalked over to Matt.

"Look at me." It was Prowler's voice, but not. He knew he should step back, but he was loath to give up full control of his body.

Matt slowly raised his head, eyes almost swollen shut. Prowler used his fingers to pry open the one that was in better shape.

Prowler felt his teeth lengthen even more, his eyes sharpen, and his face change slightly. And the nails, or rather claws, were shocking.

"There, that's better. See me, Matt, see what I am. Tell me the truth, and I'll let Ghoul over there end you nice and quick. Lie or refuse to talk, and I will eat you alive. Slowly. Painfully."

The ammonia scent of urine joined the coppery smell of blood.

"I ... I don't know his name, man, I swear. He paid me ... to-to take a smoke break. I thought he was just going to steal some money or something, not hurt anyone."

That statement did not calm anyone in the room.

"So, you were okay with someone taking from the Kings? I've gotta tell you, Matt, that's not helping things. We know what he looks like, but you gotta give me something not on the camera feed, and this can all be over for you."

"I don't know, man, he didn't give me a name." Prowler snarled and snapped his teeth in the man's face.

"Prison ink," Matt blurted. "He had some prison ink, okay." When Prowler didn't back away, Matt added, "There was another dude waiting in the car. One who was a regular here until he skipped on y'all." Matt's voice rose higher, then fell. "Travis, man. It was that Travis dude and the dude with prison ink."

And there it was. Matt had chosen how he wanted to die.

Prowler rose back to his full height and nodded at Ghoul to end the man before he and Monster strode from the room.

"I'll talk to Darcy in the morning." Prowler

yawned. "I'm going to head out now." He wobbled on his feet, absolutely spent.

Wolf was curled up sleeping already. The partial shifts and shared control exhausted them both. He should've stepped back and given Wolf control, but he just wasn't ready for that.

"You okay, Prez? You look like shit."

He barely managed a smirk at his brother. "Just tired as fuck." He rocked back on his heels again.

"Whoa." Monster caught him before he collapsed. "You're not riding. You're sleeping here."

"No. Home. Cass."

Monster must've understood. Prowler was slightly aware of getting loaded into a cage and the being put to bed with his brothers debating over undressing him or not.

After that ... nothing but black.

8

TAYLOR

Prowler said he loved her. Three words she never expected but wanted more than she'd realized. Well actually, it was just two—love you—but who needed the I? It was obvious the speaker was the I. Love you was efficient.

She giggled. Literally giggled to herself as she headed out of her half-open garage, barefoot.

"Nope." She tiptoe-hopped back as soon as her feet practically caught fire. Her drive was paved in lava.

"Duh, Tay, it's Vegas." Once inside, she slipped her now decidedly cooler tootsies into some slides. She planned to just pop over really quick and tell Prowler ...

What? What did she plan to tell him?

Love you too?

The whole wolf thing is …

"What the fuck?" she asked herself before she opened her front door.

Did he really admit to being a werewolf?

"That's impossible. Shifters aren't real." Taylor paced back and forth, talking to herself. The clop and shuffle of her slides on the hardwood floor created a soothing rhythm.

"I mean, they're hot as hell in books, but real? Nah. If shifters are real, someone would've seen them by now. Surely the government would … not tell us shit if they knew. But Booktok. Yeah, they would've definitely tracked them down, humped them silly, and posted all about it."

She laughed again, but this time it was more hysterical, less giggle.

"Hysterical—that's a sexist fucking word. Like only women get a little crazy now and then. Why not testiria? Men get crazy too." Ugh, she was losing her ever-loving mind.

"Deep breath, you're getting off topic, sister. Why not just look him in the eye and talk about it? Surely if it was even the most remote of possibilities, I'll be able to tell face-to-face."

Opening her front door, she saw Prowler

hugging his ex. This time, he wasn't an inactive victim, but the initiator.

Taylor closed the door before she jumped to conclusions. They share a child, for fuck's sake. She refused to live in a perpetual state of jealousy. Not only would that destroy her soul, but it was also a relationship killer. If they were going to make a run at being a couple, there had to be trust.

That would start now. As much as it hurt, she had to try. "It's not right to make Prowler pay for the trust another broke."

Taylor repeated that to herself over and over until she felt it. There was only one thing to do—make a list. Taylor couldn't explain it, but she found comfort in lists. She was sure her therapist would circle it back to her childhood and taking control now after the trauma she suffered then. It seemed everything in therapy, up until recently, circled back to that.

"Ha, look at that. I just saved myself a two-hundred-dollar session, Dr. Fayne."

When she heard Prowler's bike roar to life and fade away, she texted Cass.

Taylor: Wanna come over and stuff our faces with vegan ice cream and watch Jay and Silent Bob?

Cass: Not tonight. My stomach doesn't feel so hot. Raincheck?

Taylor didn't like that Cass was sick. She worried.

Taylor: Are you running a fever?

Cass: No, just blah. I think I ate something bad … maybe carob. LOL

Taylor: Hardy har har. Anything I can do?

Cass: No, I'm just going to chug some pink stuff & sleep.

Taylor: Okay, chica. Feel better & if anything changes, let me know. Just a call away.

Cass: (puke emoji) (poop emoji) (bed emoji)

Cass: (heart emoji) U (smooch emoji)

Taylor couldn't help but smile. Cass was the

best. Definitely one of the best perks of being in a relationship with Prowler.

> Taylor: Back atcha (heart eyes emoji)

Grabbing her laptop, Taylor opened a new Word document.

Setting it down, she snagged some wine and snacks from the kitchen and settled in for some deep soul searching.

She titled the document, *To Prowl or Not to Prowl.* She thought it was funny.

"Okay, Tay." She took a healthy sip of wine, then cracked her knuckles. "Let's start with facts."

- Fact - His eyes reflect light weird.
  - Fact - He does growl.
  - Fact - His teeth sometimes look longer.
  - Fact - He sees and smells things others can't.
  - Fact - I love him.

Taylor paused after that sentence. Seeing it in writing made it feel that much more real. She kept going, but the list devolved from proving or disproving the wolf theory into something more akin to pros and cons.

But once the wine was in charge, red blend controlled the keyboard, not her.

- Fact - He's an animal in bed.
  - Fact - He has an ex who wants him back.
  - Fact - His daughter is awesome.
  - Fact - He is in an MC surrounded by women.
  - Fact - He said he loves me.
  - Fact - He has secrets, lots & lots of secrets.
  - Fact - I love him.
  - Fact - I typed that already.
  - Fact - He was cozy with his ex earlier.
  - Fact - I wanted to rip her hair out for touching him.
  - Fact - I wanted to rip his hair out for touching her.
  - Fact - You have to trust those you love.

She stared at the last sentence followed by the flashing cursor, taunting her to write another sentence. One she found almost impossible to write.

The people she'd loved and trusted most in her life had done their fucking best to destroy her. For a long time, they'd succeeded, or rather she'd let them succeed. Once she broke the cycle, she'd sworn to herself never again.

Never fucking again.

If she never trusted, then no one on God's green earth could destroy her like that.

Never trusting meant never loving again.

It wasn't like Dr. Fayne hadn't told her that a thousand different times and a thousand different ways, but she just refused to take it to heart. Refused to make herself vulnerable to that kind of pain ... until Prowler.

Letting him into her bed and her heart was the best and worst thing to ever happen to her.

Best because she had so much to gain, and worst because she could lose even more.

If Prowler broke that trust—not just her suspicions and jealousy, but truly broke it—she would lose herself. All that she'd rebuilt after every man in her life had tried, Prowler would most certainly succeed.

That thought put the whole shifter thing into perspective.

With the willing suspension of disbelief, the shifter thing didn't bother her. In fact, if it were true, and if they existed, that made everything better actually. If the romance books and movies are to be believed, shifters are faithful. In most cases she'd watched or read, they were physically incapable of hurting their mates. No cheating, no beatings, no violence directed at their mates.

In one book she'd read, it made them physically ill to touch another or hurt their partner.

Successful relationships, at least the ones she'd read about because the good Lord knew she hadn't seen one up close and personal, started with honesty.

Prowler had secrets, and he'd have to share them with her, but that meant she had to share hers too.

No one knew all of her story, not even Dr. Fayne. Sure, some people knew some, others knew more. Obviously, the perpetrators knew some, but no one knew it all.

Like how one of her acts as Mykayla Barton

was trying to end her life, only to change her mind and voluntarily commit herself.

For some reason, she was ashamed of that. Mental health shouldn't be taboo. Needing help shouldn't be so secretive people go to such lengths to hide it that it disrupts their lives, but they do.

At first, she thought it was just a thing, and she told a coworker she thought was a friend. It didn't take long before no one on her shift would meet her eyes. They avoided her. Quit inviting her out. When she heard them laughing and calling her Cray-Cray Tay-Tay, she confronted them. Her ex-friend ran crying from the break room, and the manager fired her, believing she went "postal" in the break room. When in reality, all she'd done was call them catty bitches with crotch rot.

After that, she knew to keep that shit secret.

With shaky fingers, she typed

- Fact – Tell Prowler everything.

Typing it gave her anxiety.

Everything was a lot.

A LOT.

It was from family members with boundary

issues to using a man she didn't love to get away from that.

It was picking the wrong men repeatedly and allowing them to lay hands on her.

It was him knowing she used to be Mykayla Barton, and that Taylor Norton found her way out of a cycle of abuse with legal prostitution.

Everything meant *everything*, and that scared the holy shit out of her.

Setting the open laptop on the coffee table, she grabbed the bottle of wine. Fuck the glass.

After polishing it off, she curled up on the couch, hugging her bookish throw pillow like it held her together ... and cried.

She cried for all she'd lost and for the little girl who had to grow up too fast. After those tears were exhausted, she cried in sheer relief.

There was something calming about sharing her story with someone, someone she could trust. It was like a physical weight was being lifted from her. One she didn't realize the weight of until she'd decided she would unburden herself.

Fuck, had she known that was what it would feel like, she would've found someone long ago to unload on. But she knew that wouldn't have worked. Somewhere deep down she just knew that. It had to be Prowler.

I was always meant to be with Prowler.

That thought struck her. From the minute he'd moved in across the street, she felt a pull to him. He'd barely looked her way, but she didn't suffer the same affliction.

She kept her distance because she didn't want to get tangled up with another bad boy, but she looked. He was a rebel, even with his fucking trash cans. He repeatedly put them in the wrong place, and she knew from experience that they would skip his garbage, so every night before collection, she'd move his cans. She thought he'd get the hint when his cans were moved the next day, but no. He kept doing it.

One time they'd been putting them out at the same time, and she kinda went a little feral on him about can location and collection.

Yeah, not her finest Karen moment, but his eyes flashed with what she'd thought was a reflection from the sun. He looked at her differently from that moment on. His blue eyes got all seductive and irresistible. That was the first time he invited her to his bed, promising her the time of her life.

Boy, had it been tempting, but she refused to be ruled by her pussy. That went on for weeks. Each and every time, she gave him a reason why not. The next time he'd asked, he'd led with a counter-reason to their last exchange.

If she said she didn't date bad boys, next time he'd point out he wasn't talking about dating.

She doesn't sleep with bad boys ... he wasn't talking about sleep.

They were neighbors ... he'd move.

It was kind of their thing, and it was a comfortable routine. Until she'd said she didn't do relationships, and he countered with offering an arrangement with no relationship possibility.

From that day on, there was a tick-tock in her head. Counting down the seconds until she'd eventually give in.

She knew it. He knew it. Hell, anyone on the street who saw them knew it, but they enjoyed the back and forth.

Prowler enjoyed the chase, and if she were honest with herself, she enjoyed being his prey.

One more check in the *'shifters may be real, and Prowler is probably one'* column. She chuckled as she drifted off to sleep, dreaming of wolves and her future.

An annoying ringing was trying to pull her from the arms of dream Prowler. Dream Prowler with his, *"You are mine, Taylor. Mine to love, mine to pleasure, mine to command."* His voice was guttural and growly. His eyes absent of blue. *"Suck my cock like a good girl, and I'll reward you with my mark."*

"Whoa." She bolted upright, the pillow landing on the floor. She felt around the couch until she located her phone wedged between the cushions.

Through sleepy eyes, she saw it was Cassidy calling. Instantly awake, she slid her finger over the screen.

Not bothering with a greeting, she blurted out, "How are you feeling? Stomach worse?"

"Not exactly." Cassidy's voice sounded off. A little fear mixed with something else.

"What does that mean, Sassy?" She gentled her tone. Concern coursing through her.

Cass whispered, "I got my period."

Taylor didn't respond, waiting for Cass to elaborate. A surprise period sucked, but it wasn't the end of the world.

"I don't know what to do," Cass added.

How could she not know ... oh.

"You mean your first period?" Taylor had

never really given it much thought. She guessed she'd just assumed Taylor had already hit that milestone. Taylor herself didn't get it until later than the other girls at school, but she'd chalked that up to her home life.

What was she supposed to say? Congratulations? She was so far out of her depth. She didn't want to screw up, but—

Cass interrupted her wandering thoughts. "Don't give me an oh, you're becoming a woman speech or make it about your first time. If I wanted that, I would've told Mom. Please, just be all Taylor about it."

She could do that. Being Taylor was what she was good at.

"Okay, I'll come grab you, and we'll get you situated with a heating pad and the things that shall not be named." She spoke in a Dumbledore voice. "Then we'll make some red Kool-Aid, paint our nails, you guessed it, red, and watch Carrie while eating chocolate. Sorry, no pun for the last one, but how does that sound? Taylor enough for you?"

The suppressed laughter that echoed through the phone said it was.

"That's exactly what I need."

"Be there in five."

After ending the call, Taylor ordered some period essentials with a shopping service that would be there in twenty. Taylor herself only had tampons and overnight pads, neither of which were fit for a teenager.

Heading up Prowler's drive, she noticed that Allie's car was still there. The bottom dropped out of her stomach.

Trust those you love, she reminded herself.

Punching in the code, Taylor entered on silent feet and went straight to Cass's room. It was empty.

"Cass? You in there?" she whispered at the bathroom door.

"Yeah. I don't have anything," Cass whispered back.

Cracking the door just enough, Taylor passed an overnight pad to Cass. "It's not ideal, but it'll do to get across the street. You'll have a variety to choose from in a few minutes when my order arrives. Do you have clean underwear in there?"

"Yeah." Cass closed the door. "How does this thing work? I was going to Google it, but I was afraid I'd get hit with creeper fetish sites."

Taylor suppressed a laugh. The kid was probably right on that one.

"When you open the pouch, it kinda peels off,
exposing a sticky strip. Stick that to your underwear
and just pull them up. While you're doing that, I'm
going to let your dad know where you are."

"Please don't wake him. I'll be mortified, and
he'll go into that weird dad mode. Just leave him a
note."

"Okay, kiddo."

Tiptoeing back into the living room, she
grabbed a pen and paper and jotted a quick note.
She was going to leave it on the counter but didn't
want to worry him if he realized Cass was gone
before getting to the kitchen. Deciding his pillow
or nightstand was best, she crept down the hall.

Moans started to fill her ears, and her blood
chilled.

Trust those you love.

She tried like hell to swallow the lump in her
throat, but it wouldn't budge.

With a trembling hand, she opened his door
ever so slowly, and the moans got louder. Feminine moans of pleasure, to be exact.

The only light came from the plug-in air freshener plugged into the far wall, casting the couple on the bed in silhouette. The note fluttered to the floor as she watched Allie undulating atop the man she loved.

Her back was to the door, with one leg thrown over a prone figure on the bed.

Allie breathlessly whispered into the dark. "Oh, Riley. You feel so good."

A masculine half-groan, half-sound of agreement followed. Taylor closed the door and retrieved the note from the floor.

She loved.

She trusted.

She broke.

Dashing away tears that escaped even though she fucking ordered them to stay put, she almost ran Cass over.

"Ready?" she asked a little too clipped as she slapped the note on the counter.

"Yeah. Taylor? What's wrong?"

She got herself together before turning. Hell, she'd lived in a perpetual state of suck it up and don't let them see you cry since she was Cass's age. What was one more night? She could push her heartbreak aside for Cass. Tonight was all about her, not Taylor. Tomorrow she would break down and make some life changes.

She couldn't live there, not after that. Not after the worst betrayal of her life. Not after he said he loved her mere hours before. If that was his love, she didn't want it. Billy's fists hurt way less.

"Nothing for you to worry about. Let's get to my place before the delivery. I got the heating pad all ready for you."

She put her arm around Cass's shoulder and led her outside. Fuck Prowler and his growly, high-handed, alpha male bullshit. The thing she'd miss the most was right beside her. She'd grown to love Cass long before Prowler, and she'd love her long after he was just a bad memory.

Taylor sneered at Allie's car when they passed it. She'd thought it was more metaphorical than audible, but Cass proved that wrong.

"They're not together. Mom just tricked him into letting her stay in the guest room. She's never given up the idea of them getting back together, but he's not the least bit interested in getting back with her."

She wanted to say bullshit, but instead, she made a non-committal sound that was neither belief nor disbelief. It was the best she could do.

"Really, Tay. We ... talked, me and Dad. He told me a lot of things, and one of them was that you're his. So, see. Mom's tricks won't work. He loves you. I know he does."

Everything Cass just said ripped her heart to shreds. Even she'd believed his bullshit. Taylor took a fortifying breath. She'd never badmouth Allie to Cass, and she wouldn't do that with Prowler either.

Shoving all her pain and anger into a box labeled LATER, she mentally taped it closed and placed it in a closet in her mind.

"Okay, Sassy. No arguments here. However, tonight isn't about your dad or me." Then she shifted to a teasing tone and embraced Cass as they walked. "It's about you becoming a woman."

"Ugh. Whatever, Boomer," Cass responded with yet another way to call her ancient, but Taylor still joined in on a laugh at her expense.

The thought of how much she would miss Cass tried to creep in, but she pushed it down.

Tomorrow, Taylor. Just wait until tomorrow.

The delivery came just moments after they returned. While Cass was doing her thing in the bathroom with no less than five boxes to choose from, Taylor spread a garbage bag over one seat of the couch then sat on the other end like nothing was out of the ordinary. Suppressing her giggle was a little harder when Cass walked in and stopped dead in her tracks.

"Very funny. I'm dying from laughter." Walking over to where it was, she smoothed the plastic before sitting down very ladylike and tucked the heating pad into her stomach.

"Too much?"

"Nope. I expected as much from you. However, I am surprised you don't have your couch covered in plastic already. In movies from the late nineteen hundreds, all the old ladies do that."

The smirk Cass delivered was a dead ringer for her dad's, and a twinge of pain crept in. It was short-lived as Cass scooted off the plastic and tucked into Taylor's arms.

Without another word, she hit play on the remote.

They'd just gotten to the blood-dumping scene and Cass spoke again.

"I told Dad about my wolf theory."

"Oh yeah?" Taylor didn't want to dime out her dad if she didn't know he'd told her.

"Yeah, and guess what?"

A prickle ran across her neck, causing goose bumps to rise in its wake.

"What?"

"I was right."

And there it was. The elephant, or rather shifter, in the room.

It was true. Shifters existed. Prowler may be a dirty rotten manwhore who can't keep his dick in his pants, but he would never lie to his daughter.

If Taylor's world hadn't been turned upside down by what she'd witnessed in his bedroom earlier, the realization that werewolves were real would have done it.

"So, your dad is a wolf." It wasn't really a question.

"Yeah, and so are Kansas, Monster, Golden, and Hunter."

"Interesting."

She dropped her voice low, almost in wonder. "But Bulldog is a bear. An actual freaking bear, and can you guess what Ghoul is?"

"What?" What could be more fantastical than an MC full of shifters, including a bear?

"A mountain lion."

Taylor had to laugh at that. The jokester of the bunch was a mountain lion.

"Oh, that's rich. I am cueing up the cougar jokes as we speak."

Cass sat up with a look of worry in her blue eyes.

"You can't. Well, not yet. Only family can know they exist. It's like their code. I just told you because, well, you are family to me. And as soon as you and Dad get together officially, and he claims you, you'll be even more family."

Taylor's brain couldn't even process her words because she was too busy reminding herself there would be no more joking with Ghoul or any of them.

"Okay. Mum's the word." She tucked Cass back into her side and stared at the TV, not really watching.

That brought on a whole other host of questions. Questions she didn't want to ask. Questions she wouldn't ask because the answers may sink her too deep into their world to get out—and get out she must. She couldn't stay and watch Prowler with woman after woman.

He'd said she was his, but he never used the word mate. Oh god, what if Allie was his mate? Taylor could no more watch that than watch him go through women searching.

Isn't that what the men in her books did? They knew instantly who their mate was. She and Prowler had been having sex for months, and he never went feral over her or tried to bite her.

That realization was like a gut punch. He knew Taylor wasn't his mate, but he'd kept sleeping with her anyway. Did that mean when he found his mate he'd toss her aside, no matter how many times he said he was all in?

She really, *really* couldn't do this.

"Taylor?"

"Yeah?"

"Who was that man the other day? The one who came to the door during Tombstone?"

"Technically, he's my brother, but I don't consider him that because he's not a good person. If you ever see him around, run, Cass."

"Oh good. I mean about him being your brother and not about him being a bad person."

"Why?"

"Because Dad was asking if I knew who it was."

"How did he know about that?" It was a stupid question. She'd seen one of his brothers out in front of his house when Travis left.

"The front camera picked it up, and he was jealous."

Wait, what?

Great. Not only was that a violation of her privacy, but he was jealous when he was the one sleeping around.

Double standard much?

Her first thought was to just sell her house and break away from everything Prowler, shifters, and Kings of Anarchy.

Besides, now that Travis knew where she lived, it probably wasn't the worst idea she'd come up with.

"Thanks for everything, Tay. I don't know what I would've done without you. I wish you were my mom," Cass confessed sleepily.

Tears sprang to Taylor's eyes. Another thing she never wanted but couldn't imagine life without now that she'd had it.

As Taylor sat there with Cass asleep against her, she revised her plan.

Why should she sell her home for a man?

It bothered her that her mind was reverting back to running instead of fighting.

Fuck that. She would fight, but not for Prowler. She'd fight for herself.

She'd end things with him but come up with a way where he wouldn't try to woo her back as he did last time she tried. She'd stand firm and make him want to end it. That way, she'd still be able to spend time with Cass.

And when seeing Prowler with other women or even Allie got to be too much, or she got to be too weak, she'd spend a few nights at her rental property across town. Lucky for her, it was currently vacant.

She breathed a sigh of relief that she wasn't running. She was fighting, just on her own terms.

9

PROWLER

Prowler came awake to Wolf howling and thrashing to get out. Which made zero sense because their woman was ... smelling all wrong.

IT'S NOT OUR MATE, YOU FUCKING MEAT BAG.

Wolf growled with a ferocity that Prowler had never heard before.

Jackknifing up from the bed, Allie went flying off him.

It was true. It wasn't his mate trying to wring pleasure from him. He and Wolf both had been so exhausted they were practically comatose, and Allie had taken advantage of his state of stupor.

"What the hell, Riley?

"FUCK," both man and wolf roared. Wolf's pain manifested itself in physical agony for Prowler, nearly doubling him over.

"Get your shit and get out."

"Riley, you can't kick me out." Allie stood naked and unapologetic, meeting his gaze. Big mistake, Wolf took that as a challenge. "If I go, Cass goes …" She walked her fingers in the air. "All the way to Tucson with me. And who knows when you'll see her—"

Her words were cut off by a half-shifted paw to her throat. "You go to your room, pack your things, and be waiting by the door until the lawyer arrives. Then you'll sign any fucking papers he puts in front of you, and then I don't want to lay eyes on you again. Do you understand?"

The fear he saw in her downcast eyes was real, and this time he could smell it on her. She gasped, and Prowler shifted his hand back, releasing some of the pressure on her throat.

She nodded her compliance, and her words were resigned.

"He'll kill me if I run away."

"I'll kill you if you don't."

He shoved her toward the door, and she went.

"What are you?" Allie asked in a shaky voice but didn't turn back to look at him.

"I'm what you made me. Now go."

That was the first time he realized how much resentment he had toward her.

He took his first life because of her.

He had a wolf because of her.

And his biggest regrets in life were because of her.

But she also gave him his greatest joy, so he was deeply conflicted.

Now that they'd bonded, he didn't see Wolf as a negative.

Allie was in the guest room banging around. He wondered how they hadn't woken Cass. He pulled on his jeans and didn't bother with boxers or even buttoning them. He headed toward Cass's room to peek in on her. It was empty.

Maybe she was already awake and just ignoring the ruckus. She was an early riser, and it was sunup.

He didn't find her in the living room either. Just as he was about to freak out, he spotted a note on the counter.

Riley,
Cass is with me. I'll let her explain the impromptu sleepover, but give her time, don't hound her. I promise it's nothing to be concerned about, just girl stuff.
Love, T

Love.

She wrote love. He gave a little howl. He could feel Wolf's joy, but it was tainted. *He* felt tainted.

Wolf?

Nothing.

"Wolf?" Prowler spoke aloud, but Wolf's only response was a snarl followed by a whimper. Prowler's muscles were still contracting and contorting in pain. He could tell it came from Wolf, but he didn't know what to say to bridge the chasm that had so recently closed but now reopened larger than ever before.

I'm sorry. I ...

Prowler was at a loss. He didn't understand Wolf's pain. He was a man of action, not talk anyway.

What Wolf needed, what he needed, was his family together in his house and Allie out of sight.

Grabbing his phone, he called Langley, who answered on the first ring.

"Where are you?" Prowler asked as soon as Langley picked up.

"You're up, good." Langley spoke over Prowler's question.

"I need you here now."

"Good thing I've been in your driveway for thirty minutes waiting for the lights to come on."

Prowler didn't care for lawyers, but Langley was okay. The club took care of him, and he in turn took care of them.

Prowler threw open the door before the man could knock and stalked back toward the kitchen island with Langley on his heels.

"Allie. Get out here." Within moments, Allie appeared with her travel bag and eyes cast down.

There was a touch of regret for how harshly he treated her, but not for her—for their secret. She now had firsthand knowledge that he was more than just a man.

Prowler shoved a pen in her hand, but Wolf snarled and twisted his muscles when she got within two feet of them.

"Ah, Ms. Powell, sign here. And here." Langley flipped pages, and Allie signed. When she set the pen down, she turned to Prowler but not looking him in the eye.

Good.

"Can I see Cass at all?" She sounded genuine.

Prowler thought.

He didn't want to keep Cass away from her mother, but he couldn't look at her. Couldn't ask Taylor to look at her, even though she didn't know Allie was in his bed trying to fuck him while he was practically unconscious.

Wolf scoffed, and then snarled, fangs bared ... toward Prowler.

What the fuck.

Prowler raked his hand through his hair and paced.

"Langley, can you print our standard NDA?"

"Don't need to, brought one with me." Langley pulled another document from his briefcase. The MC had an NDA everyone had to sign who wasn't a member but visited the clubhouse. It not only covered what happened on the property but any member activity as well.

By default, that covered shifter stuff too. Not

that it would keep all mouths shut, but it gave most people pause.

No one wanted to fuck with the Kings unless it was worth it. And they made sure it was never worth it.

Prowler nodded, and Langley handed Allie the pen again.

"If you sign and agree to tell none of my secrets. I'll not only let you have time with Cass, I'll send monthly payments until you die."

She turned her gaze up to him for the first time. Greed glittered in the eyes he once found attractive. Now they only repulsed him.

"Even if I remarry?"

Prowler nodded. "Even then. It will be enough that you won't ever have to work. You can—what was it you said? Realign your stars. But I'm serious about never seeing you again. Someone else will be a go-between with Cass. If I see you again ..."

He let the threat hang because it wasn't really a threat. Wolf would rip her limb from limb, and Prowler didn't know if he could stop it. Hell, he could barely hold him back being so close to her. Prowler didn't understand his anger, his agony. He just knew that Allie had to go. Luckily, Langley pretended he was shuffling papers and not paying attention to his words.

"I'm as good as gone." She smiled, and it felt greasy. Like he'd just been played and maybe he had.

After signing, she picked up her bag and sashayed out the door.

Wolf needed to watch her leave so Prowler followed her to her car. Once she cranked it and put it in gear, she rolled down the window.

"Head's up, there's a man looking for your whore, and he's bad news." She reached her hand out and dragged her nails along the exposed skin between his zipper flaps. He caught her hand, lightning quick, and stopped her downward exploration. She ripped it free easily, as Wolf couldn't stand to touch her.

"By the way, I love the new piercing." Her gaze dropped to his denim-covered crotch, and she licked her lips. With those parting shots, Allie pulled out of his driveway and left.

He'd recently gotten it done as a surprise for Taylor. Thank God for shifter healing. She hadn't had a chance to see it yet, but his ex had. That was not good. It made him sick to think that ...

It was then he'd realized how thoroughly he'd

been played by her. She wasn't going to Tucson. She hated her fucking parents.

And time with Cass? That was a fucking joke. If she cared at all, she would have wanted to say bye and then realized she wasn't there.

Fuck.

Speaking of Cass, his gaze was following the progress of Allie's car and spotted Cass and Taylor walking up the drive.

His smile fell when he took in the look on both their faces. The two people he loved most in this world were disappointed in him. He could smell it.

"Hey, Jellybean."

He held his arms out to his daughter, but her gaze dropped.

He zipped his pants and held them out again. She accepted his embrace but whispered, "Dad, how could you? With Mom?" That fucking broke him.

Yeah, he knew how it looked, and he would explain to Cass later, but right now his Wolf was pushing against him to go to Taylor. The pain coming off her was gagging his senses. It was bitter and pithy, but then he smelled something else ... blood.

The morning had been too overwhelming for

him and Wolf already. He couldn't hold back the snarl.

"Are you hurt?" His gaze snapped from Cass to Taylor. Taylor's gasp told him it was Wolf's eyes staring at her and not his. But Wolf wanted nothing to do with Prowler's anger. He was whimpering in the corner. They were completely out of sync again, but Prowler was in charge.

"Why is my daughter bleeding?" he asked as he stalked toward Taylor. "Your note said it was nothing bad. You lied. To me."

Wolf came from his corner, trying to burst free, to stop Prowler, but instead of listening, he cowed Wolf. His daughter was hurt, and he couldn't deal with that. Not now, not ever.

"Oh my god, Dad. This is so embarrassing." He heard his daughter retreat and the door close.

"Answer me," Prowler ordered. "I smell her blood."

"God, you're such an overbearing jackass. She got her period, you fucking idiot. Here." She thrust a bag against his chest, and both man and beast calmed at the contact. Her touch was everything.

He didn't speak, just kept staring at Taylor.

"It's a period survival kit. Once she decides what she likes, remember it so you get the right ones. Nothing worse than being bloated and cranky and not having the one thing you need be right."

She turned to go, and Wolf snarled at Prowler.

God damn it.

"Taylor, wait."

She turned and crossed her arms over her chest. Prowler couldn't control his gaze when it dropped to her tits. She was practically presenting them to him.

When she cleared her throat, he shifted his eyes to her, and there was pain there.

Pain and anger. He could smell it now that he wasn't focused on Cass.

"It's not what it looks like."

"Whatever do you mean? The part where your ex spent the night or the part where she tried to give you a goodbye hand job from her car? Or maybe the part where you couldn't even bother to dress to tell her bye?"

"None of that is true, Taylor, just give me time to explain."

"So, your ex didn't spend the night?"

"Yes, but not like that."

Both Taylor and Wolf called him a liar without words.

"Well, as far as her getting handsy, and you being half dressed, the evidence is clear, and there were witnesses."

"I know how it looks, sweetheart, but come in for coffee and let me explain. I have so much to tell you, and I want to start this off with full disclosure."

Before Taylor could respond, Langley walked up to them. "I've left the other things you requested on the counter. I'll get this back to the office and then file these."

"Thanks," he muttered as Langley dipped his head to Taylor before striding to his car, briefcase in hand.

As soon as he drove off, Taylor took a deep breath. "Look, Riley, I was wrong to be so overly emotional about Allie. You can sleep with whoever you want, and it doesn't concern me. It's obvious we are better off as neighbors, so let's just shake hands and go back to that. This thing between us has run its course."

"The fuck it has." Prowler grabbed her arm when she turned to leave. "You're mine, Taylor, and I'll never let you go."

Wolf spoke to him for the first time since calling him a meat bag.

Gentle. She's our mate, and she's in pain.

He loosened his grip almost instantly at Wolf's voice, and Taylor turned.

"Wow. It is true. Shifters are real."

She didn't speak with fear but with dissipating disbelief and shock.

Prowler flashed his eyes, and a sad smile crossed her face.

"That's right, sweetheart. And I can make those romance novels you read a reality if you let me," he purred.

"That's fiction, Riley. This is reality. And in reality, we are friends who used to sleep together. Nothing more."

"Bullshit," he roared. The calm her gentle acceptance of his kind had brought him completely vanished. She was still trying to leave him. "You're mine, Taylor, and we hold on to what's ours. Don't your romance novels cover that?"

Her mouth contorted like she was holding back tears. When she laid her hand on his cheek, he burrowed into the touch, and so did Wolf.

She took a deep breath and wouldn't meet his eyes.

"I'm so sorry, Riley. I was using Allie as an

excuse because I fucked up, and I couldn't face it." She took another deep breath and dropped her touch. "It was me. I slept with someone else. I broke the agreement, so see? We have no choice but to end things. I can't be yours. Your kind needs fidelity, don't they?"

She turned and walked away, and Prowler roared.

"Who?"

The sound of Wolf chanting coupled with the roar of his own blood was too much to bear. Her scent was even more bitter. Taylor stopped but didn't turn.

"Who did you sleep with? He's a dead man." Prowler growled, Wolf gnashing his teeth to break free and mark her.

Taylor remained silent, even with the alpha emphasis he put on his words.

"Was it the fucker at your door the other night? The one who picked you up?"

"Yes," she answered, her voice wavering, but she still didn't turn around. "And by the way, reposition your cameras. It's a violation of my privacy to have them pointed at my property."

With that, Taylor continued across the street, and Wolf broke free right there in his driveway.

His howl pierced the atmosphere before he bolted to the backyard and leaped over the wall. After pacing back and forth until the sun was high in the sky, Wolf curled up next to Prowler's favorite chair. That's where he stayed until his daughter appeared and opened the glass slider to let him in.

After padding into the house beside Cass, he leaped up on the couch next to where she'd plopped down. Having fingers buried in his fur, stroking and petting him, was a new experience.

"Why?" His daughter dashed away tears. "Why would you do that to Taylor? You told me she was your mate. You love her, and I know she's in love with you, so why did you let Mom come between you?" Her tears had turned into a full-on waterfall. "I thought we'd be a family. I thought ..." Cass trailed off.

He wanted to change and tell her ... what, he didn't know, but he wanted to hold her, comfort her, something, anything, but the sun had already set, and Wolf wouldn't concede.

Give me my body. Prowler commanded.

No. You fuck everything up, so maybe I should stay in charge.

She wrapped her arms around his ruff and just

cried into his fur. When her tears were dry, she let him go and stood. As she headed to her room, she turned back to him.

"I love you, Dad. I love you too, Wolf. I'm disappointed in you both, but I love you."

The words shot an arrow straight to his heart, but the disappointment and sadness stung. He'd give anything to make her happy. He just didn't know how. The thought of Taylor with another man, writhing under him, was too much. He couldn't erase it from his brain. It was playing over and over. How could he live like that?

He couldn't. He'd have to find a way to live without her, no matter how painful that would be. He had no choice. Wolf may be able to forgive, but the man couldn't. As much as he loved her, and he did fucking love her, he just didn't believe he'd ever get to a place where sleeping with someone else was forgivable.

But you wanted her to forgive you.

Wolf finally spoke to him.

I didn't fuck Allie.

Keep telling yourself that, meat bag, and we'll never be at peace.

I DIDN'T FUCK HER.

Prowler shouted in his own head. It was weird

being in fur and speaking to Wolf. It had never happened before. When Wolf was in fur, Prowler was ... sleeping for lack of a better explanation. Unaware of what was going on for the most part until it was time to shift back.

Our mate saw her in your bed.

What?

She came to the door and watched as that slag rubbed her gash against your dick, trying to get you hard while moaning your name.

Prowler didn't remember that at all.

Why didn't you fucking stop her?

I tried, meat bag, but you exhausted us by not truly letting me lead when sharing your body. That way of sharing control will eventually kill us if we don't bond. It suppresses us both more and more until ...

Taylor saw him and Allie in bed. She must've thought...

Thought you fucked her, yes. Her pain was crippling. Of course, you didn't have to feel it.

Prowler did not like being a passive observer in Wolf's head.

Now you know how I feel.

Wolf could hear his thoughts apparently. Thoughts not directed at him.

We have to bond. Until we do, I think I'll stay in charge.

I thought we had.

Yes and no, but any bonding we had was broken by you.

Prowler knew somewhere deep down that Wolf was right. He'd broken it, and he had to be the one to fix it. They needed to bond for good. The problem was he didn't have a clue how to make it happen.

Since that issue didn't seem to have a ready solution, he focused on things that maybe he did have an answer to.

While he didn't know if he could forgive Taylor, he still loved her and didn't want to cause her undue pain.

Well, on a positive note, I didn't fuck Allie. We have to find a way to tell Taylor so she doesn't hurt.

Who said you didn't fuck her?

You. You said she was trying to get me hard. Not that she got me hard. Therefore, no sex.

Wolf just whimpered like a wounded animal, and pain radiated through their shared body.

Prowler swallowed the lump in his throat, and it felt like a cannonball hitting his stomach. As much as he didn't want to, he tried to remember.

If Wolf could see through Prowler's eyes when in the back, maybe he could tap into what Wolf saw while Prowler was in the back.

He remembered dreaming of Taylor. Dreaming of her lying on top of him. How her skin and weight felt, but the dream stopped there when Wolf started beating the shit out of him from the inside before taking over. The next thing he remembered was Wolf throwing Allie off him, but he didn't remember anything else.

Prowler was skulking through Wolf's memories when he ran into a vault. Instinctively, he knew he'd find what he was looking for in there. He threw his body weight against it repeatedly and nothing.

Wolf shouted in his mind.

ENOUGH.

Wolf, let me in.

No. You don't need access. Those are for me and me alone. Wolf warned.

I need to know what happened. I need to remember. Prowler begged.

You don't need to remember because I will never forget. I will always remember last night as being unfaithful to my mate, my heart, regardless of what your mind or body did or didn't do. So, it doesn't matter how or if you remember it.

Wolf whimpered before continuing.

You do not need the look on her face when she opened that door burned into your mind for all eternity as it is mine. Even if I get a new companion, I know that memory will linger.

Wolf sounded absolutely devastated. His voice was unlike he'd ever heard it before. Prowler was too. And not just for his current situation, but for Wolf. When he'd told Prowler only some memories remained from past companions, he'd assumed just special ones. But that didn't seem to be the case.

Wolf was protecting him, shouldering the bad memories alone.

Hours more passed with silence between man and beast. He remembered Cass patting him good night as he slept on the couch in wolf form. Wolf still not giving up his body.

With the sunrise, Wolf finally spoke again.

You have to forgive her. We must win her back.

Fuck he wanted to. He wanted to so badly, but he just didn't know. Maybe once they killed the fucker, he could find a way to let it go.

We will wither and die without her. And it won't take as long as you think.

Kansas says—

Kansas doesn't know. We are different. We cannot survive ... and neither will Taylor.

If it was a choice between losing her forever or forgiving her, there was only one choice.

With that understanding, something changed between them. Prowler would be hard pressed to describe it, but they became one while remaining two.

They bonded.

They bonded over pain and impending demise, but mostly they bonded to save Taylor. Wolf had proven himself as a protector, but who protected him?

Prowler certainly hadn't. He tolerated him at best, used him, and locked him away at worst.

Prowler made a vow to protect Wolf, even from himself.

I will protect you and our mate. This I vow to you. Apparently, that was what Wolf needed to hear.

Wolf gave Prowler his body and retreated, but not as he had in the past. Prowler felt his presence, and it wasn't intrusive. For the first time, it didn't feel foreign. It felt right.

And I will protect you and our mate. This I vow.

Prowler hurriedly got dressed before making a quick breakfast.

"Jellybean, breakfast?" he called as he set the plates at the table

She emerged from her room dressed for the day.

"Don't you mean brunch? It's a little late for breakfast."

"Call it what you want, but you need to eat. I made a tofu scramble." He didn't add *for protein.* He assumed since she was, well, you know, that protein was the answer.

They ate in relative silence until Cass had taken her last bite of toast.

"Look, you're right. I do love Taylor, and we'll work it out, but I can't promise we can settle our differences right away and be the traditional family, Jellybean."

No matter if he could get over it or not, he was compelled to protect her and Wolf. That meant figuring out a way to make it work. Maybe he could sleep through the tough moments, like intimacy. Then he remembered his vow, that would be using Wolf, and he wouldn't do that anymore.

"Traditional is overrated, Dad. Besides, when have we ever been traditional?"

His daughter's statement pulled a laugh from him.

"True."

He didn't fucking know how he was going to manage, but he would. He would give Cass the family she wanted and Wolf his mate and him his ol' lady if it killed him.

No pressure.

He realized he was no longer at odds with Wolf but instead with himself.

The look in his daughter's eyes hurt more than the physical pain Wolf inflicted on him, that he'd inflicted on Wolf.

"I have to be honest, Jellybean, Taylor may not want to be with me."

"Why not?"

"Because."

He was not about to explain adult problems to his fourteen-year-old child. Not only that, she adored Taylor and badmouthing her was a recipe for disaster.

"Because why?" Cass took a tone with him, and he didn't like it one bit.

Fuck. It was so much easier as Wolf. Cass

seemed taken with the furry side of him. Now, she looked at him with that look. The one she'd normally reserved for her mother—and that was a knife to the chest.

"So, you cheated, she will forgive you."

Without thinking, Prowler blurted out ... "It's not my infidelity, but hers, that's the problem."

He'd fucking done it anyway, he badmouthed Taylor. Cass and Taylor had a beautiful relationship. One that transcended what he had with Taylor or what Cass had with her mother.

Cass stared at him wide-eyed.

"Way to deflect." Her disappointment was thick and heavy in the air between them. He could practically taste it.

He took a deep breath because he was getting heated, and he didn't want to add his relationship with his daughter to the pile of things that were fucked up.

"Listen, Jellybean. The thing with your mom was, well, it looked a lot worse than it was." He had to dance around it somehow, while still being honest. "She was not invited to my bed, nor was I awake while she was in it."

Her forehead furrow relaxed. "You promise?"

Prowler nodded.

"I knew she was up to something when she packed a bag."

In hindsight, he should've known too.

"Be that as it may, Taylor came to the same conclusion as you did. So, we will have to address that."

"She'll forgive you, Dad. Taylor has the biggest heart of anyone I know." Cass stood and came to his chair, wrapping her arms around him from the side. He leaned into her embrace.

"I know, Bean, but I don't, and I don't know if I can forgive as easily."

"Why ... Wait. Is this about that guy on camera you were snarling about the other day? The one you wanted me to ask about but didn't tell me to ask about."

Prowler laughed. His daughter had his number. "For the record, you're far too perceptive. Let's drop it for now. This is a me problem, and I'll work it out."

Cass let him go and scooped up his plate then hers, walking both to the sink. "Well, then, I guess I won't tell you who he is, since I have to drop it." Her voice lilted.

Prowler leaped from his chair. "You know who he is?" It took every ounce of restraint not to command her to tell him. But he'd already promised himself he wouldn't do that.

"Yes, and she most certainly didn't sleep with him."

His first emotion was relief, his second was disbelief. How could his daughter possibly know that for certain?

"Who is he?"

She put down the dish towel she was wiping her hands with.

"Her brother. But she told me to run if I ever see him, so he must be some piece of work."

The emotions that flooded Prowler and Wolf were too many to process and too intense to contain.

They howled.

Long and loud and victorious.

They had a mate to claim.

He kissed his daughter on the cheek and jogged—no, ran—across the street.

She didn't answer the door. He stalked around back and hopped over the wall. No sign of her. He sniffed around.

Her scent wasn't fresh. She wasn't home.

Using the gate, he exited the proper way and

pulled his phone from his pocket. His call to Taylor was rejected. She'd fucking blocked him.

"I'll just sit out front and wait her out," he muttered to himself.

That's when he noticed her garbage cans were out.

Trash wasn't for five days, and she was anal about her cans. Both timing and placement, so he could only draw one conclusion.

She wasn't coming back for at least a week.

"Fuck."

10

TAYLOR

After putting her trash out, she packed a bag and left for her rental house. It was small and sterile, but it would do for the respite she needed.

The wound that was Prowler was too raw. Her hope was, with time, she could spend all her time at the house that she loved and the pain of seeing Prowler with another woman wouldn't be as sharp.

If only she were his mate, like in fiction, and everything could've been unicorns and daisies. He wouldn't ever cheat if she were.

Rationally, she knew that if Prowler found his mate, the kind of love that was in her favorite shifter novels, she could eventually move on. She wanted that for him. Hell, she wanted it for herself too.

It just couldn't be Allie. That she couldn't stomach. She told herself she was a one-time thing for whatever reason because the thought of that vile woman with him was too much to bear. And poor Cass, she was not a fan of her mother. She especially hated the idea of her parents together.

No, if it was Allie, she would definitely sell her dream house and move.

She'd lose both Prowler and Cass, and that would suck.

The first thing she did after getting settled into her rental was text Cass to see how she was feeling. Taylor didn't discuss the things that had happened or tell her she wasn't staying at her house. Cass didn't need to be in the middle of what was going on between her and Prowler.

As much as she wanted to ask about Prowler, she didn't, even when Cass had indicated that he was in wolf form. That made her question if her lie was worth it after all. Would he have come after her if he could have?

The answer was deep in her bones.

No.

Prowler was not the type to accept that another man had been in her bed. That's why she let him think the worst of her.

She was still wrapping her head around Prowler being a wolf and that shifters were real, but it made sense. She'd thought over the last few months how animalistic some things he did were. The way he stalked instead of walked. The way he used certain words. How he rubbed his cum onto her skin to mark her.

Humans were ridiculously naïve if they thought they were the most superior species in their vast universe. Hell, Taylor had no problem believing that aliens were out there, just not little green men. Personally, her fingers were crossed for blue men from a very cold planet.

But humans certainly were not alone, and if that could be true, then why not shifters? The legends had to start somewhere. That was the only reason the whole thing didn't freak her out more than it had, because on some level she'd always believed in things like that.

After getting cleaned up, she donned her uniform and headed for work. She'd gone in a few hours early, hoping to catch Claire before she left. Taylor was thinking of taking the next few days off, to sit around the rental and feed her broken heart into submission. She hoped Claire would be down to cover a few shifts.

With that handled, she fixed her face and stepped out onto the casino floor.

Throughout her entire shift, she felt like someone was watching her, but she couldn't see anyone creeping in the crowd. In fact, the whole crowd was pretty tame for once.

It felt like the shift that would never end, but thankfully, it did.

One of the small pleasures in life was getting out of her skimpy outfit and putting on a baggy tee and comfy sweats after a shift.

But pulling off her heeled boots was downright religious. After getting dressed, she stood.

"These sneakers feel way too good. My dogs were barking."

"Same, sister, same," one of the new girls said. She didn't know her name, nor had she realized she was in the room.

"Right? Nike is missing a huge market by sticking to athletes. They could market to waitstaff and dancers, really any working-class girl on her feet all day in heels, and they'd double their profits."

"Preach." New girl closed her locker and turned.

"Oh, I'm Taylor, by the way. We haven't officially met." She shouldered her bag and extended her arm. "Welcome to the Himalayas." Taylor did Yeti's voice from Monsters. Inc, but her coworker seemed puzzled.

"It's from a movie. I'm a little weird like that, sorry." Taylor dropped her hand.

Way to make it awkward. For some reason, the exchange had her holding back tears. Cass would've got it, rolled her eyes, but then laughed. Maybe even made an old lady retort.

"Oh, I know that. I'm Nikki. I just thought you said your name was Taylor."

"Yeah, I did. See." She pointed to the masking tape with TAYLOR N. stuck to the front of the locker behind her. "That's me."

"I thought it was Makayla. That guy must've made a mistake."

Taylor's blood ran cold. Fucking Travis was at her work again. It had to be.

"Guy?"

"Yeah, some guy tipped me a hundred dollars and asked about you. Called you Makayla."

Alarm bells were going off in her head. Travis knew she had changed her name to Taylor and wouldn't need to ask about her unless he was trying to send her a message.

"What else did he say?"

"I don't remember to be honest. It was loud, and up close his breath stunk of beer, so I kept leaning back. But he did mention something about how you looked different from when he knew you."

Her breath locked inside her lungs. It couldn't be Billy. No way he would've found her. Maybe one of his buddies found his way to Vegas again, that's all. Those guys fall out all the time. Billy got rid of his friends for any minor infraction.

That's all it was.

Or at least that's what she tried to convince herself of because the alternative was unthinkable.

She put on her happy face like she'd learned over the years, no matter what turmoil was going on under the surface. "Ready to head out?"

"No, you go on. I'm going to grab a bite."

Taylor nodded and opened the door. As

expected, security was right there waiting to walk them out.

"Nikki's not coming just yet."

"Cool," he answered and followed her to the garage and all the way to her car door. She was not making the same mistake as last time.

"Be safe, Taylor." He tapped the roof of her car and walked off before turning back. "Oh, and avoid the Charleston exit. Just heard there's an accident that has it backed up." With that he waved and watched her back out.

All the way to her rental house, paranoia had her in a death grip. Every car that pulled in behind her was surely following her. In Vegas, that was a lot. No street ever seemed completely void of traffic.

Her rental was in a mid-sized older community that was experiencing a revitalization. When the houses were redone, they ended up practically eliminating the driveways for a few hundred more square feet, so it was all street parking. Since her unit had been vacant for a few months, one of her neighbors had taken to parking in front of her house.

It was annoying to have to park a bit away, but at least she wasn't in those god-awful heels. She was walking on the sidewalk in front of her unit when a man started jogging her way and calling out.

Immediately she dropped her bag and took up a fighting stance.

"Whoa." He stopped and raised his hands. "Didn't mean to frighten you. My wife wanted me to come move the car. She said someone was staying here now. When I saw you walking, I realized I should've done it when she asked instead of waiting. Sorry about that."

Taylor not only breathed a sigh of relief, but she may have even laughed about it a little.

"Sorry about the Tyson stance, but I mean, you came out of nowhere in the dark. I could barely make out your shadow."

"Yeah. That's on me. Bad choice." He bent to retrieve her bag. "That and these three streetlights have been out for months. My wife has called the city a million times, but, as you can see, still in the dark."

"Thanks." She re-shouldered her bag.

"Anyway, I'm moving my car now if you want to move yours up." He unlocked his door. "Have a good night, um?"

"Taylor."

"I'm Miguel. Me and my wife Maria and our boys live over there in the blue house. You should come for dinner some night, Maria makes some mean tamales. She'd love to meet you. We just moved in, and she doesn't know anyone in the area yet."

"Nice to meet you, Miguel. And the first thing you should know about me is I never turn down good food, so don't just offer to be polite. Warn Maria though, if the tamales are as mean as you say, she may never get rid of me."

Miguel laughed. "Maria is going to love you."

The whole exchange lightened her mood. Maybe her time spent there wouldn't be so bad. Keeping busy was a bonus. If she was eating tamales with Maria and Miguel, she wouldn't be wondering what Prowler was doing.

Who he was doing.

After setting her things down on the counter, she went to move her car. Having it almost a block away was fine for the night, but having to hoof it tomorrow when the sun was out and it was over one hundred wasn't her idea of a good time.

"Fuck," she cursed as she rolled up next to the curb in front of her house. She hopped out to check her rims. She had gotten really close to the curb. Reaching for her phone, she realized she'd left it in the house.

"Guess I'll have to assess the damage in the morning," she groused before heading inside. Realizing she'd left the door ajar when she went to move her car, she double-checked that she locked it before she went to draw a bath.

When she leaned over to adjust the faucet, she froze. There were footsteps behind her.

"I always did like that view of you, Mykayla."

Billy's voice triggered something inside her. For years she froze at that sound, made herself small, but not anymore. She whirled around, swinging and kicking. Not having a clue where he was, she didn't care. She'd already proven that she could and would fight back, even with Billy.

Her fight was short-lived when he headbutted her, rocking her back before spinning her into a bear hug. That's when she saw her brother.

Travis.

"Hello, sis. Long time no see."

The sight of Travis renewed her fight. When he approached her, she twisted and flailed trying to loosen Billy's hold, but it was no use.

"Open up, sweetheart." Travis tipped a water bottle to her lips with a hand in a black brace.

Fighting like hell not to ingest whatever it was, Taylor kicked Travis frantically while turning her head.

Travis grabbed her breast, digging his fingers in but standing far enough to the side she couldn't kick him.

"Listen to me, sister," he sneered. "You either open up and drink it now, or you'll open up screaming when I shove my cock up your ass, and Billy can pour it in then. You're choice."

Being raped by Travis was a real and present threat since she was a teenager. It was her nightmare fuel, so she complied, swallowing the warm water with chunks of bitter pill bits in it, until he pulled the bottle away.

At that point, if he was going to do vile things to her, she hoped whatever he'd given her knocked her out.

They dragged her to the bedroom and tossed her on the mattress. When they started duct taping her, she tried to fight again, but it was two against one. She was completely overwhelmed.

"What the fuck is this?" she asked as they wrapped duct tape around her thighs.

Both men just looked at her like a bug under glass.

"This? Well, that depends on who you ask." Travis kept wrapping, tearing the tape with his teeth and moving to her ankles.

They had taped her legs *together*, over her sweats, so at least rape wasn't their primary intention, and she found a small measure of comfort in that. Especially since that used to be Billy's kink, taking her when she really didn't want him to. The harder she'd fought, the harder he'd gotten.

Funny how one's mind works when faced with the unknown. With her biggest fear alleviated, she could analyze the situation for what it was, not from a place of defense.

"What's going on?" she asked again since her previous inquiry went unanswered. She needed to understand, to have a sense of control.

"If you ask me," Billy sneered, "You're not worth much more than what's between your legs and what you took when I got locked away."

"What I took? Dude, you're fucking delusional if you think that shack in the desert had anything worth taking."

He got in her face so fast, she recoiled out of habit, but he didn't hit her. Instead, he pulled her hair, wrenching her head back, and spit in her face. She gagged.

"Oh, there was, and you fucking know it. My stash was gone when I got out, and so were you. I don't think that's a coincidence."

Taylor's brain was spinning. He'd gotten out shortly after she'd fled. He was only out three months before getting locked away again, that time for years.

When she left their home, if you could even call it that, she took nothing but the clothes on her back, her cigar box, and her piece of shit car that gave out within the week.

"Do you mean the one hundred and fifty bucks in the cigar box that I earned in tips? Because that's all I took with me."

"No bitch, I don't mean that piddly stash of cash you had in a cigar box, I mean *my* stash," Billy roared and drew back his fist. Taylor screwed her eyes shut and braced for impact, but it never came. Travis stopped him.

What the fucking hell alternate universe was she in where Travis protected her?

"Easy, big guy. I told you. You only get paid if I do, and I won't get paid if she's all bruised up."

Billy turned on Travis

"You promised I'd get payback."

"Yes, I did, and you will. But I can't deliver that if the Kings don't want to pay for damaged goods."

"Payback isn't just about the money and coke she took. She humiliated me when she left. That can't go unanswered."

"I said I would get you your money. As far as any other retribution you're after ... well, that will be between you and the Kings, AFTER we get paid."

Billy was pissed at Travis's answer. Taylor knew that look, and Travis would be smart not to turn his back to ... wait.

"What?" Taylor asked in disbelief. What the hell did the Kings have to do with her brother and her ex? It made zero sense. Other than Travis and a ridiculous scheme to get money. No way Prowler knew her ex or her brother. The world just wasn't that small.

"Oh, sweet sister. You didn't think I found you by accident, did you? Wait, actually I did. And this whole time you were blaming Terry the goody two-shoes for ratting you out."

"If Terry didn't tell you where I was, how did you find me?" She cut her eyes to Billy, who was seething in the corner. He was the more dangerous of the two in his current state.

"I think it was divine intervention. I owe those bastards in Kings a large sum of money. And do you know they had the gall to threaten me? Sent their muscle after me even. I was a good customer, always paid my debts. But I get in a bind once or twice, and they turn into savages."

Taylor was hella confused because none of what Travis just said answered her questions in any way, shape, or form.

"Get to the point already." This from Billy in the corner.

Travis snapped his head in Billy's direction. And issued a rebuke Billy didn't take well. Hell, Taylor could've told him not to poke the bear.

Turning back to her, he continued. "As I was saying, they came after me, so I decided to turn the tables and go after them. I followed each one home and watched and learned. Imagine my surprise when I saw you sneaking out of the President's house in the wee hours of the morning. It was like God himself was smiling down on me. So, I bided my time. How I wish I'd had the time to get you alone with that young one. Oh, how much fun we could've had."

His mention of Cass stoked a fire deep inside her.

"If you even think about touching her, know that I will fucking hunt you to the ends of the fucking earth with my last breath. You will not touch her."

"Don't threaten me, sister, you won't like the results. Besides, she is plan B. But you're plan A, so do your part, and I won't need to enact plan B."

She was losing patience with Travis. He was monologuing just to hear his own voice, and whatever he'd given her was starting to kick in.

"How did you come to owe an MC money in the first place? They run a bar and a hotel. What? Did you take the towels when you checked out?"

His laughter bounced off the walls. "Oh, that's rich. Do you not know anything about the men you spread your legs for?"

She cut her gaze to Billy. "Obviously." She turned back to Travis. "Why don't you tell me before I break the other one?" She stared pointedly at his wrapped wrist.

It was an empty threat, but she wanted him on the defensive, and he hated any shortcomings or failures being pointed out.

"It's not broken, just sprained." He sneered but

stood up from the foot of the bed to pace. She preferred the distance. Without him on the bed to feel her movements, she worked her charm bracelet down. A part was caught in the tape, but it was loose-fitting, so she was able to contort her fingers and grab a charm.

Score, lightning bolt, the sharpest one.

She made a series of pokes and saws while Travis paced and spoke.

"The Kings don't just own a hotel. They own a brothel. Picture it—the wife and kids are in the hotel pool while the husband is getting his dick sucked just a stone's throw away. It's brilliant really."

If Travis thought that would shock her, it didn't. He didn't know she'd been a working girl herself at one time, and you can't turn away a client just because he was married. However, the fact that the Kings owned one, hidden in Vegas no less, was a surprise. Despite what people like to think, prostitution was in fact illegal in Vegas and Clark County.

"The bar—well, that's just a bar, a run-of-the-mill dive with video poker. But it's where people go to find the Kings and secure a loan or an invite to their casino."

That paused her little lightning bolt. If Travis was to be believed, Prowler and the Kings were into some heavy illegal shit. The one thing casinos hated more than cheaters was illegal competition.

She wanted to keep stabbing and sawing at her duct tape. Free herself, kick their asses, and call Prowler to warn him about Travis and to protect Cass.

She also wanted to hear more of what Travis had to say. She wanted to keep him talking because something just wasn't adding up. Travis and Billy knew each other from when they'd been a couple, but since when did they work together?

Billy had only tolerated Travis to piss her off. He loved making her miserable, and Travis was one way to do that. However, it was Travis's loose lips that got Billy pinched one time, so he told him to disappear and never come back. It was the one and only thing Billy had done in their relationship that made her happy.

More than knowledge, her body craved sleep. It was giving in to whatever Travis had given her.

"What was in the water?"

Travis waved her off with his bandaged wrist. "Nothing more than the painkillers they gave me for this. I just need you not to be hysterical while I contact your lover. Damn pills suck anyway, so it'll wear off soon."

She drifted off to sleep. She had no idea how long she'd been sleeping, but it was light outside, so for a while she surmised. She vaguely remembered being awoken, allowed to relieve herself, and made to drink more pill water.

When she woke the last time, she heard Travis's voice, but not a responding answer. When she peeked through her lashes, he was on the phone. She didn't want them to drug her again, so she feigned still sleeping.

"I want to talk to your president."

Pause.

"It doesn't matter who this is. Get me the president."

Another pause.

"I'll call back in twenty. If he doesn't answer, I'll start carving parts off his girlfriend until he does."

Time passed slowly, pretending to sleep. She wanted to look around, to be on the offensive, but it was too risky. She did, however, ever so slightly keep that lightning bolt moving.

"Wake up, sweetheart." She blinked her eyes

open to see Travis standing by her head with the phone in his hand on speaker and ringing.

The ring abruptly cut off with Prowler's voice.

"Where the fuck is she, you bastard?"

"Mykayla, say hello to your lover." He held the phone closer to her face.

"Prowler?"

"Fuck, babe, are you okay? Where are you?"

"I'm sorry, protect Cass. T—" That was all she got out before a hand covered her mouth. She didn't even notice Billy standing there. She tried screaming through his hands, but it was no use. She should've blurted out the address, but all she could think about was Cass.

"Taylor! Taylor!" She heard Prowler shout before Travis took the call off speaker and put it to his ear.

"Listen, Prowler. If you want Mykayla, oh I'm sorry, you know her as Taylor. Whatever her name is, if you want to see her in one piece again, you'll have two hundred and fifty thousand dollars put into locker 17 in the men's locker room at Top Notch Gym on Rainbow. Lock it with the lock that's inside."

Prowler's response was so loud, Taylor heard it through the phone.

"I'm going to eat your heart, motherfucker," Prowler threatened.

"So, is that a no on the money then?" Travis asked with that air of superiority he always had. "I guess I'll start with those luscious tits of hers. I'll put them in a box and send them to you."

"WAIT," Prowler shouted. "Don't hurt her. I'll get you your fucking money, but how will I get my mate back?"

Taylor's heart caught in her throat. Could she really be his mate, after everything that had happened? Maybe romance novels had it wrong, and mates could cheat, but could she live with that? She most certainly couldn't live with it being an ongoing thing, but she could forgive him for his one indiscretion, if he could forgive her for the one he thought she'd committed.

She loved him so much she had pretty much forgiven him. She just needed to lick her wounds, and well ... that didn't work out so well.

She turned her head as much as she could and cut her eyes back to Billy to see if the word mate registered, and he had a curious look on his face. Shit, Billy was the last person who needed to be privy to that secret.

It didn't appear Travis caught it. He started

speaking over Prowler as soon as he said he would get him his money.

"Once I have the money, I'll give you the address where she'll be safe and sound, waiting for her knight in shining armor to save the day. You have until eight, or it's bye-bye breasts."

With that, he hung up, not giving Prowler a chance to respond.

"You're gonna wish it was a knight in shining armor when a King in dusty leather shows up, asshole," she mumbled against Billy's hand.

When she'd heard the anger and determination in Prowler's voice, a sense of comfort washed over her. Bone deep, she knew that she was looking at a dead man as soon as Prowler had found her—and he would find her, of that she had no doubt.

Billy let her go and stood. "Do you really think the Kings'll pay two fifty for her? She's just some gash. Hell, they got better than her working for them. That Darcy, damn. I might have to have another go at her."

Travis turned to Billy, tapping his temple with his finger.

Travis was either incredibly brave or stunningly stupid.

"Think, monkey, is any pussy worth your life? We get this money drop from them, we disappear. You stay in town, and you're a dead man. But hey, once you get your fifty back, you do you. I'm gone though."

Billy slapped his hand away and spoke through gritted teeth. "Fifty's not going to cut it anymore, Travis. I want half."

"Half? For what? I did all the legwork, and I called you in out of the goodness of my heart. I could've done this without you."

Travis called Billy on her. She already wanted to kill him, but that made her want to kill him twice.

"I gave you two guys to do your dirty work, and you killed them. You owe me," Billy accused.

"Your guys were useless. You should thank me for ridding you of them."

"Fuck you, Travis. I want half. You only owe the Kings a measly fifteen grand, add my fifty. We agreed to ask for one hundred just to square up, but you wanted more and changed the game. Now I want more, and I'm changing the game."

Travis pulled a gun and stuck it in Billy's face. "You're not in charge. I am. You'll take the fifty and be grateful I gave it to you instead of blowing your brains out now and keeping it all for myself." Travis really was arrogant enough to think he had the upper hand, but he was woefully outmatched by Billy.

"And just so you know, Mykayla knew nothing about your stash. Rookie move keeping it in the same place all the time."

Billy was a crazy motherfucker, and Taylor knew from experience that shit was about to go south real fast. She could practically see his temper rise and hear the blood pounding in the vein at his temple. The one that visibly pulsed right before he'd swing on her.

"You don't have the balls," Billy taunted and leaned closer to the gun, puffing up his chest.

When Travis didn't respond right away, the smile that slowly curved Billy's lips gave her flash-backs. Travis had crossed a line. One he wouldn't come back from if she were a betting woman.

Lightning quick, Billy's hand came up and batted the gun away. It landed with a dull thud on the carpet. He rushed Travis and was on top of him, pounding his face in the blink of an eye.

Taylor swallowed her scream, not wanting to draw Billy's attention, and continued to poke away at the tape. She was making progress. Just a little bit more, and she'd be able to hook it on something and pull down to rip the tape.

Without warning, the dull thuds of Billy's fists on Travis's face stopped, and the sputtering started. She'd had Billy choke her unconscious enough times to recognize the horrifying sound.

She refused to watch as Billy choked the life from Travis. She couldn't even bring herself to feel sorry for the bastard. What did that say about her?

Billy stood with bloody hands and a gleam in his eyes, stalking toward the bed. Grabbing her legs, he started removing the tape from her ankles.

"What ... what are you doing?"

"Whatever the fuck I want to do."

He started on the tape at her thighs.

"After I have you, I'll go find that pretty little thing Travis couldn't shut up about. I'll fuck every one of her holes bloody, then I'll take her with me when I split. They'll never come after me if I have the president's little girl."

Before she could scream no, the bell rang, and Billy covered her mouth. "Don't make a sound," he rasped.

The bell rang again, followed by a knock. Whoever it was, wasn't leaving.

"I'm going to remove my hand, and you're

going to tell them you're coming, understand?" She nodded.

"If you do anything to tip them off, I'll kill whoever it is, and it will be your fault." She nodded again.

When Billy removed his hand, she shouted. "Be there in a minute."

Billy finished removing the tape from her legs, and when he got to her hands, he tsked. "You'll pay for this." He indicated the tear in the tape.

"Now go." He pulled her from the bed and shoved her forward. "Get rid of whoever it is and don't let on, and don't fucking run or else ..." He let the threat hang with a bullet to the brain motion.

Taylor smoothed her hair as best she could and answered the door while Billy was just out of sight, watching.

"Oh wow, Miguel." Her heart sank when she saw his wife and two kids in tow.

"Maria insisted on meeting you and bringing you some tamales."

Maria held up a covered plate. "Hi, when Miguel said he met you the other day, I couldn't wait. I hope you don't mind."

The other day? How long had she been drugged?

"Of course, I don't mind. Who are these strapping young men?"

"This is Aiden and Isiah."

Miguel raised a steamer pot. "We can help you set this up if you want."

"Yes. I forbid you from heating my tamales in the microwave."

As much as Taylor wanted to keep Miguel and his family far away from Billy, she couldn't just kick them out, that would raise suspicion.

"Of course, come in. I hate to be rude, but it will have to be a quick lesson. I have to shower for work." As the family filed in, she shifted nervously on her feet, trying to block the view down the hallway, but had to relent and join Maria at the stove for her lesson.

"It is really simple. Just put a few inches of water here. Place this on top. Then once it boils, place the tamales here and put the lid on. In ten minutes, perfect tamales."

"Seems simple enough. I will definitely be noshing on these tonight after work, and I'll return the pan and the dishes tomorrow."

"We're sorry, are we interrupting something?"

Miguel asked as he glanced around, seemingly taking in everything.

"No, not interrupting, but I'm so far behind. I took a nap, and well, it was one of those naps that was supposed to be thirty minutes, but lasted hours, and now I'm late."

She was rambling, but she had to get these precious people, who wanted nothing more than to be friends, out of the house where a dead body and a madman were just feet away.

"Of course, of course." Maria gathered her sons, looking dejected.

"How about Saturday I come over and cook dinner for you guys, to make up for me rushing you off tonight? Spend the day getting to know each other."

Her offer made Maria smile, and that made her feel better. Miguel had a shrewd gaze about it but relented. "Of course. You take care, Taylor, and in the meantime, if you need anything, anything at all, we're just a shout away." The way he projected his voice made her wonder if he knew something. She blanked her face as best she could.

She breathed a sigh of relief when she closed the door behind them. She looked at the clock on the microwave, and it was not quite seven.

For a moment she thought of going for her phone, but knew Billy would make good on his threat, and she would not let Miguel and Maria's family pay for her mistake.

She wasn't taped, and that was something. She had a fighting chance, but only if …

Just then, Billy came from the bedroom, grabbing her by her hair and dragging her back.

"Now we're going to have some fun."

11

PROWLER

The second the realization hit him that Taylor was gone, he called emergency church.

"I need everyone to drop everything and find my mate. You." He indicated Kansas and Boogeyman. "Check every type of record you can. Public, private, fucking Reddit. I don't care. Hack her cell phone, her smartwatch, whatever it takes."

"Did someone take her?"

The question scraped at Prowler's heart. Of course, his brothers were ready to go to war for him. But admitting that she'd run and why was going to be a jagged pill to swallow.

"No." He sank back into his chair. "She ran ... from me. But now. Now, I'm not so sure. Call it a gut feeling."

There were murmured questions all around. None of which he wanted to answer. Thankfully, both Kansas and Boogeyman, despite their questions, were already typing away on their laptops.

"Listen, I ... she caught me in a compromising position. I—"

Before he could continue, questions flew at him from all directions.

"How could you ..."

"Why didn't you ..."

"You could've tracked ..."

It was deafening.

"ENOUGH," he roared.

The entire room fell silent. He didn't want to hide anything from his brothers, but he was ashamed.

"Look, the sharing of control Wolf and I did the other day exhausted us both because I wouldn't relent. I was dead to the world. Ghoul had to drive me home and pour me into bed. Later, Cass called Taylor to come over and, um, help her with a delicate situation."

That was the best he could do. It was hard enough to face the fact that his little Jellybean was growing up without blurting it out to his brothers. Besides, his daughter would be horrified if she knew he talked about her period in church.

"According to Wolf, that's when Allie climbed into my bed. Taylor saw it, and well, it looked exactly the way that bitch wanted it to look. Regardless, she took Cass to her place and handled it. She didn't let on to my kid that anything was wrong. Fast forward to the early hours of the morning, and Allie was at it again." He swallowed the lump in his throat.

"This time it wasn't for show. Wolf was able to wake me, and it got ugly. I threw her out after she signed over custody. Of course, she couldn't just fucking leave without a performance, and there were Taylor and Cass looking at me with heartbreak and disgust. It appeared bad, especially coupled with what Taylor had seen before."

That look still haunted him, and not just Taylor's. He never wanted his child to look at him with disappointment again. He pulled himself together and continued.

"Anyway, long story short, she said she cheated, and I wolfed out for a few days."

"Fuck, Prez, you sure she's your mate then?" Kansas looked up from his laptop to ask.

"Yes, she's mine, and don't question it again.

She lied because she was hurt. Cass told me the man on the feed was her brother, not her lover."

Prowler pulled out his phone. He had the video saved from the night he'd been at her house. Because he planned on killing the man who kissed her. Now he planned on killing him because of what Cass had told him.

"Maybe she's just somewhere licking her wounds and will be back when she's ready. You should give her some space." Of course, Bulldog would think that.

"I don't know. I thought that too, but she quit answering Cass's texts and calls, and that's not like her. She is always there for her, day or night." When he got her back, and he would get her back, he would let her know how much that meant to him. He'd pretty much had just taken it for granted because how could anyone not love Cass, but Taylor went above and beyond for his kid.

"Call it my gut, call it the mating bond in waiting, call it whatever you want, but I just need to lay eyes on her and know she's okay." If she was okay, and space was all she needed, then as much as it would kill him, he would give it to her. He just needed to know she was safe.

"Got something," Kansas declared. "She owns

a property on the other side of town. A rental from the looks of it. Currently vacant, but the listing got pulled." He scrunched his face and scrolled. "About the time your girl went into prey mode."

Prowler could've jumped for joy. It wasn't very likely she was there, but it was something. A lead he could be busy following instead of hating himself for hurting her.

"I'll head out in ten to check it out. Ghoul and Bulldog with me, just in case."

He slid his phone down the table. It was a long shot, but something about the timing of her brother showing up set alarm bells off in his head after what Cass had said.

"Take a look at that and see if you recognize him. It's Taylor's brother, but he damn sure didn't act like any brother should toward his sister. Plus, she told Cass to run if she ever saw him."

Ghoul had just grabbed the phone and turned to Prowler when Boogey declared, "Good news, her cell is at that rental."

"See, she just needed—" Kansas started, but Chef interrupted him.

"That's fucking Travis." Chef's statement was punctuated by the door flying open, with a wind-blown Monster standing there panting.

"Someone has your ol' lady."

The room exploded into chaos. It was fucking bedlam.

"QUIET."

This time, Prowler himself felt the alpha command in his voice, and a few of his brothers not only bowed their heads, but one took a fucking knee.

He and Wolf were well and truly one. Not only was it obvious in his brothers' reactions, but it was also obvious because he was still in skin.

No one spoke, not even Prowler. The clicking of the keyboard ceased, and the only sound he could hear was the buzz of the lights.

Thoughts of what Chef and Boogey had said fled in the wake of those five words.

Someone has your ol' lady.

"Speak."

No one needed any clarification who he meant.

"Got a call on the book line."

Before Monster said another word, Prowler snatched the phone.

"Where is she?" When he got no response, he looked at Monster.

"They'll call back in twenty. Said you must

answer, or they start carving. That was about fifteen minutes ago."

He turned on his road captain and had him by the shirt. "Why didn't you call me then?" Prowler spoke through the canines he purposefully lengthened.

"Because." His eyes flashed. "I didn't want to waste a single second," Monster snarled back. "My office is thirty minutes away on the best of days. I just made it in half that, then threw my sled to the fucking ground, all so you wouldn't miss the fucking call."

Monster's wolf had issues, and it showed in times like these. Prowler dropped his eyes to the silver cuff he wore to keep his feral wolf in check. Yep, issues.

Prowler took in Monster's appearance, and it was obvious he was traveling pretty fast without a helmet. His hair was plastered back, there were random blood specks and nicks on his face, and he wasn't wearing his cut. Fuck, his brother went above and beyond for his girl.

Releasing his shirt and cupping the back of Monster's head, he brought their foreheads together. "I'm sorry, brother. Thank you. I owe you."

He'd just turned to the rest of the room when the phone rang.

"Where the fuck is she, you bastard?" Probably not the best way to answer the call, but Prowler was done. No matter what this fucker said, they were heading to that house as soon as the call was finished. That's where her phone was, so that was better intel than anything the dead man talking would say.

"Mykayla, say hello to your lover." The next voice he heard was Taylor's.

"Prowler?"

"Fuck, babe, are you okay? Where are you?"

"I'm sorry, protect Cass. T—" Her words turned his blood to ice, and then they were abruptly cut off.

"Taylor! Taylor!" Prowler screamed at the phone.

"Listen, Prowler. If you want Mykayla, oh I'm sorry, you know her as Taylor. Whatever her name is, if you want to see her in one piece again, you'll have two hundred and fifty thousand dollars put into locker 17 in the men's locker room at Top Notch Gym on Rainbow. Lock it with the lock that's inside."

"I'm going to eat your heart, motherfucker," Prowler threatened.

"So, is that a no on the money then? I guess I'll start with those luscious tits of hers. I'll put them in a box and send them to you."

"WAIT. Don't hurt her. I'll get you your fucking money, but how will I get my mate back?"

"Once I have the money, I'll give you the address where she'll be safe and sound, waiting for her knight in shining armor to save the day. You have until eight, or it's bye-bye breasts."

With that, the fucker hung up.

"That was Travis," Ghoul declared. "I'd recognize his nasally voice anywhere."

"That, and he called her Mykayla. That means Taylor is the sister who fell off the face of the earth a while back." Kansas observed.

"Couple that with what she told Cass and what she just said about protecting Cass, and I'd bet he's the reason why," Chef added.

It was a lot to take in at once, and Prowler had to remove his emotions from the equation and operate with a clear head.

"Chef, join Creedence at my place. One of you inside with eyes on Cass." With nothing more than a nod, he complied with Prowler's order.

She'd hate it, but he wasn't taking any chances with her safety.

"Bulldog, Kansas, and Ghoul with me. No colors."

Prowler shucked his cut and turned to leave, knowing his brothers would follow. When they strode out the door heading for the van, he saw Monster's bike lying on its side at the end of a skid, headlight still on.

When Prowler turned it off and picked the bike up, he noticed some blood on the ground. Of course there'd be blood. His brother threw down his bike to make sure he answered the call when it came.

"Hey, Boogey," he shouted back inside.

"Yeah, Prez?" Boogeyman stood in the open doorway.

"Patch Monster up and snatch that cuff off him for a few hours.

"Will do, Prez."

Prowler made a mental note to get Monster's bike fixed for him out of his own pocket, not club coffers. It was the least he could do.

The four men were armed and loaded into the van. The drive to Taylor's rental seemed to take forever, but only complete morons broke traffic laws when they had a shit ton of unregistered weapons.

Pulling into the neighborhood, they could see it was street parking only.

"Perfect," Kansas said. "We can do a drive-by and assess without it appearing out of the ordinary if we circle back."

They did just that.

"There's her car," Prowler pointed out.

"We got walkers at three o'clock and a Kravitz at ten." Everyone turned to where Kansas indicated. There was a family just heading inside of the blue house and a fluttering curtain on another.

"Circle around, we'll park on the street behind and come up between the buildings. No one seemed to be paying much attention over there." It wasn't fully dark, so they couldn't just pile out of the van with weapons and waltz up to the front door.

Ghoul followed his direction and killed the engine. "Too risky for guns, even suppressors would draw attention in these close quarters. We gotta go old school, brothers."

Prowler grabbed his bat, and they headed in to save his girl. Climbing the back wall gave them some cover to get the slider open. If people only knew how easy those things were to pop, they'd remember to always put the bar down or go old school and use a sawed-off broom handle. Hell, anything to keep the slider from sliding.

Prowler would have a talk with Taylor about her safety when this was all over.

As Bulldog slid the glass aside, he heard a man who was not Travis. "Now we're gonna have some fun."

Prowler didn't need another syllable or the sounds of a pained scream from Taylor to propel him into motion. He shoved around Bulldog and down the hall. There was a burly fucker dragging Taylor into a room by the hair on her head, and he saw red. If he didn't think that a snarling, snapping Wolf ripping a man's throat to shreds would freak Taylor out, he would've shifted. Instead, he tackled the fucker.

He was vaguely aware of knocking Taylor away and hoped she hadn't got hurt. He'd also lost his bat, but fuck it, he'd beat the fucker to death if he had to.

Everything happened so fast it was like he was watching it ... through Wolf's eyes. While he hadn't shifted, Wolf was definitely in charge.

And Wolf was pissed.

After a few punches, the man turned the tables. He ended up on top and landed a few good ones before Prowler heard a sound he recognized, and the man went limp.

Prowler shoved the dead weight off him. He stood and went straight to Taylor, who was holding his bat.

"Are you okay, babe?" He held her face in his hands, examining her in the low light. Other than a small red spot on her forehead, she looked none the worse for wear. "Talk to me, Taylor. Are you okay?"

When she still didn't answer, he looked to Ghoul and Kansas, who stood in the hall as Prowler and Taylor were blocking the doorway.

"All clear," Bulldog said as he joined them.

Ghoul stuck his head in to survey the scene and whistled low. "Looks like someone took care of Travis already. Let me just squeeze by you," he said as he did just that, checking pulses. "Travis is eighty-six, but this fucker." Ghoul hauled off and punched him in the face. "He's still breathing."

"No." Taylor finally spoke. "No." She seemed shocked as she shoved past Prowler.

She kicked the big guy in the nuts, and he

groaned. "No," she said again, this time low and menacing. Then she raised the bat and hit him in the face.

Every one of them recoiled, not expecting that at all.

"No." She did it again, but the third time, Prowler had to stop her. That was not a woman who was traumatized and fighting her attacker back with rage. He didn't know what it was, but Taylor was in control. Maybe she was scared.

"Hey, babe, it's okay. You don't have to be scared anymore. It's over." He wrapped his arms around her from behind.

"I'm not scared, Prowler. I'm pissed." She turned in his arms. "You have no idea the things he said he wanted to do to Cass. I told him I'd stop him, and I did."

Amid the blood and bodies, Prowler was bursting with pride and love. Taylor was made for him. He understood the fated mate, the one person perfect for man and beast thing whole-heartedly, looking at her like that. And she was going to be perfect as his ol' lady.

Some would say it was sick and twisted, but fuck it, he was sick and twisted.

He removed the bat from her hand and held it

behind him for someone to grab. The bat left his grasp, and he heard Bulldog speak. "That's blood in, Prez."

Ghoul added, "And one hell of a blood in at that."

Prowler couldn't hold back any longer. "You're mine, Taylor. My mate, forever." His lips descended on hers. It was not a gentle meeting of mouths. It was a frenzy of lips and teeth.

"Let me just scooch past you there," Ghoul said as he exited the room. Using his booted foot to move a leg, he closed the door, behind him.

"Taylor." He held her face a little too tight, so she looked him in the eyes. Eyes that were currently amber. He and Wolf were fully bonded.

"Do you accept me as your mate?"

Her pretty green eyes got sadder, if that were possible in the current setting.

"Can you forgive me for cheating?"

"I could if you'd cheated, but I know you didn't. Either way, I'm sorry for how I reacted. I should've been more understanding, especially considering ..." He let the words trail off, not wanting to say it but knowing it had to be addressed.

"So, you really did sleep with Allie? I prayed it was a trick or something."

"It was a trick, babe. Allie staged the whole thing." He was loath to dash the joy on her face away, but he had to be honest. "That time. However, the next morning she was in my bed again when Wolf woke me."

"So, which is it, Prowler? Did you fuck her or not?"

"Wolf won't tell me, but the way he acted after, I wonder if something started that he woke me up to end. Either way, I can tell you with one hundred percent certainty, I would never cheat on you willingly. Wolf would destroy me if I even thought about it."

"I love you, Prowler. That's not a secret to anyone. I can endure and survive almost anything this life can throw at me because I'm finally strong. I made myself strong. But if it takes a biological imperative to keep you faithful, I'm not strong enough for that. So tell me how you feel, driven by love, not instinct."

Fuck, he was not a man of words, and he was fucking it all up. He'd changed so much when Allie cheated on him, not just the Wolf part, but he'd walled up his heart. Taylor was worth looking behind that wall and speaking to from his heart as best he could.

"I love you, Taylor. I love how you love my daughter, how you've loved me even when we said it was off the table. I love how you make shitty brownies because it will make someone else happy when I know you take your chocolate seriously." She smiled at him for what felt like the first time.

"And I love how you look at me like you are now. Like you don't need food or oxygen, you just need me. Like I am enough to not only sustain you but to feed your soul. I love how you love me. I love you because you're you, and I'm me, and together we are the perfect we. I'll be faithful because I want to be, choose to be, and because I never want you to look at me any other way than you are right now."

"Damn," she said breathlessly. "You are like a live panty remover 3000. I literally just dropped all my eggs at once."

He kissed her again.

"And I love how you can joke when we're surrounded by all this ugliness." He laughed.

"And I love you because you can make me feel like we're not."

What he had to ask next could send her running for the hills. "Taylor. I need to mark you. Now. It's the instinct and not the romance you deserve, but I can't, Wolf can't, let you walk out that door without our scent on you a minute longer because if we mark you, we can find you, and this kind of thing won't happen again."

He took a deep breath. "I promise you all that romantic bullshit later, but right now, I need to claim you. Hard and fast."

"Romantic bullshit? You've never done traditional romance before, why start now?"

"I wasn't going to start now, babe. That was the whole point of my speech. Do try to keep up," he growled. When he lifted her off her feet, she wrapped her legs around him. He took the two steps to the bed and brought them both down.

"This is your last chance, Taylor. If you don't want to be tied to me forever, stop me. One of my brothers will see you home safe, we'll get this cleaned up like it never happened, and we can revert back to our original post-situationship agreement."

Taylor slid her hands up his torso, under his shirt before pulling it over his head.

"Could you really do that, Riley? Go back to being neighbors?"

"No," he admitted.

"Neither can I."

"I'm sorry I let this happen. It'll never happen again. I promise I'll protect you, no one—" A finger to his lips cut him off.

He made short work of their clothes before sliding down her body to kneel on the floor with her legs over his shoulders.

He nipped that sensitive spot on the inside of her thigh that he knew drove her wild. "This is the most perfect inch of skin in the world. One day, I'm going to mark it."

His tongue swirled her clit before dipping inside her sweet cunt, wrenching a moan from her. His brothers heard, even without their enhanced hearing, but he couldn't bring himself to care.

"Oh, Riley. Yes, right there. Don't stop."

Not that he needed the encouragement, but it didn't hurt. When she came with his tongue buried deep inside her, he stood licking his lips.

"Umm." Kissing his way up her body, he went to kiss her, but when she raised her lips to meet his, he backed up a fraction, just out of her reach.

"On your hands and knees, pussycat. I'm going to make you mine."

He growled his words, his canines extended and slicked with the serum he'd use to imprint his scent on her.

His mate.

It resonated differently inside him in that moment, with her luscious ass in the air as he stroked the head of his cock through her wetness.

Prowler couldn't wait another second to claim her, so he thrust forward to the hilt, ripping another moan of pleasure from her lips.

Pushing her head down into the mattress, he pummeled into her, moving the bed as he did. He'd feared hurting her during claiming with the way Kansas had described it for naturals, but Taylor was his match in every way. Even this, she was relishing it as much as he was.

"I'm coming, Riley. Oh fuck, I love you." The velvet walls wrapped around his cock started to milk him. Pulling her torso up, he wrapped an arm around her waist to hold her to him. The other still wrapped in her hair, exposing her neck to him. She was still coming when he struck. Burying his teeth in her neck as he joined her in bliss.

Kneeling on that bed, they were as connected

as two people could be. Pressed together from their thighs to where his teeth were buried in her neck. His cock still sporadically pulsing inside her.

When her flutters had ebbed, he willed his teeth back to those of a man and lowered them both to the mattress.

Instinctively he knew to lick her wound. "It'll be sore for a while." He kissed her neck.

"Worth it?" he asked.

"Totally."

Prowler pulled her tighter into his body at the blissed-out way she'd said it. His cock still nestled in her warmth.

Caressing her thigh, he joked, "Better than your lady porn books?"

Taylor turned in his arms, dislodging his cock. "So much better. I may have to burn them all because there is nothing like the real thing."

12

TAYLOR

Taylor touched the spot on her neck. It had healed into a scar, and she'd made a game of making up countless stories over the past few weeks about what had happened when a coworker or rude customer asked.

Each time it got more outlandish. Her personal favorite was a hungry raccoon at the 7-Eleven dropped down from the ice machine onto her shoulder and took a chip right out of her hand. When she took it back, the damn thing bit her.

Prowler wrapped his arms around her from behind, kissing the back of her hand that still rested on her mark. "You know that look you get on your face every time you touch my mark is the same look you get when I'm eating your pussy."

She spun in his arms. "Stop. What if Cass hears you?"

He liked how she still blushed when it came to sex talk in public. She was an absolute fearless goddess in the sack, but talk too loud in public, and she turned downright virginal.

"No."

"No?"

"Yeah, no." He moved her hand and kissed her mark. "This says I can talk about eating your pussy anytime I want to."

"This?" She pointed to her mark. "Oh, I got this on Fremont one night. Me and my girlfriends were celebrating a little too hard, and there was a homeless man and a dog. When I tried to pet him, he bit me."

"Wow, you tried to pet a homeless man? No wonder he bit you." She stuck her tongue out at him and ducked under his arms.

Prowler followed, pulling her back. "Come on. We've got time for a quickie."

"Riley Reynolds, that's a bald-faced lie, and you know it. Your quickies take twenty minutes minimum, and with traffic, we'll be late."

The ride across town was faster than expected. After killing the engine, they both dismounted.

Helmet off, Taylor opened the saddlebags and started removing covered dishes. She had to opt for smaller containers because of size restrictions, but she made it work.

"See that." He thrust his wrist in her face. "We could've had a quickie, even my version of one, and still been on time. So, you owe me when we get home."

"Home. I like the sound of that."

Taylor thought listing her house and moving in with Prowler and Cass would feel restrictive, but it didn't. If anything, she felt loved and accepted ... free. Freer than she had ever been before.

"Hey, Prez." Bulldog waved from across the street.

"Vice. How you liking the new digs?"

"I can't complain. Better than the last shithole I lived in. Of course, the last tenant left one hell of a mess, but I got it cleaned up."

"He has jokes," Taylor delivered dryly.

She wasn't quite ready to make light of what happened there, who died, how ... but she wasn't sad about it either. But make no mistake, she'd do it all over again if it meant protecting Cass. Or Prowler or any of the Kings.

They'd all welcomed her with open arms.

"We'll drop off any leftovers in a few hours."

Bulldog's grin was massive. She knew the way to that bear's heart.

"Woman, what are you doing with that one? You ever want a real man, call me."

Prowler growled, and Taylor elbowed him. "Calm down, Cujo. You know he's joking."

"I know, but I can't help it." He sounded so pouty. "Maybe if I would've gotten that quickie ..."

With that, Monster and Kansas came out of the door behind Bulldog.

"Did someone say leftovers?" Kansas said at the same time Monster spoke.

"Did someone say a quickie?"

Taylor rolled her eyes. Fucking shifter hearing. "I'm going to go ring the bell."

She made a mental note to ask Prowler why Monster still had a slight limp. Barely noticeable, but still present.

The men reassured her after the whole mate thing that they were hard to kill, fast to heal, and loved with everything they had.

The fact that Monster hadn't healed worried her.

Maria answered the bell almost immediately.

"Oh wow, here, let me help you. Come in, come in. You brought enough food to feed a small army."

"Oh, but there's more. Prowler's right behind me."

Miguel appeared and took the last of her dishes. As soon as her hands were free, Maria filled one with a wine glass.

"Come, sit." Maria beckoned.

"I'm going to go see what's keeping your ol' man." Miguel left them alone to talk.

Miguel earned the club's respect when he'd knocked on the door, with a gun tucked in his waistband while she was otherwise occupied with being claimed.

He'd told Kansas something didn't feel right when they were there, and Taylor rushed them out. Between her clothes and attitude, he came back to check on her.

She adored him for that. He had no more than a three-minute exchange with her about parking, yet he knew something was off. So even if the Kings hadn't shown up when they did, she would've had Miguel, and that warmed her heart.

Dinner with their new friends Miguel and

Maria was amazing. She'd never had couple friends before. Of course, this was the first time she was half of a normal couple. If you could call being completely head over heels in love with a wolfman MC president normal.

Her brain was turning some things over on their ride home. Some things about Miguel scratched at the back of her brain. His instincts to know something was wrong, or how he saw her walking up the sidewalk with the three street-lights out. She'd been in a complete dark zone.

"Prowler?" she asked through the helmet's built-in comm unit.

"Yeah, babe."

"You said shifters can smell other shifters, right?"

"Yeah, in most cases."

"Can you smell Miguel?"

"No."

"So, he's not a shifter?"

"I didn't say that. But what Miguel is or isn't is his business."

That was vague and non-committal.

The first thing she did when they got in the door was take off her shoes. She placed them in the coat closet, between Cass's flip-flops and Prowler's running shoes.

The picture made her smile. They were really doing this.

"What are you studying so intently?" Prowler asked from behind as he haphazardly tossed his boots in.

"Nothing."

"Good." He laced their fingers together and led her to their bedroom, complete with a new bed. She'd insisted on that.

"Get undressed, babe. I do believe you have a debt to pay." She did as he asked.

He led her to the mirror. "Fuck you look perfect, but I think you're missing something," Prowler said before he tied a soft blindfold around her eyes.

"Taylor, you're a goddess, do you know that?"

"Oh, I've graduated from babe to goddess, have I?"

"Yes." He nipped his claiming mark, and instant arousal shot straight to her clit. "You have, but it's still missing something."

She heard the closet door open, and a moment later, Prowler guided her arms through openings.

Something that felt like silk caressed her skin, hardening her nipples even more.

She almost wanted to cry. She knew what he'd just put on her, and it felt like armor, even though it was clearly satin-lined leather.

Prowler reached around and pinched them. "Fuck, you're absolutely perfect." Prowler stepped away, but it was only a moment before his hands came around her once more. He was naked, his cock was already long and hard. The new piercing teasing her back. God, how she loved that tiny piece of stainless steel.

One hand was kneading and massaging her breast. The other trailed down her stomach to the place that was crying out for his touch. He dipped two fingers inside her body, gathering her arousal. Which he spread to her clit, making the circles at the speed he knew drove her mad.

"Oh fuck, Riley. That feels so good." She had no sooner said that, and his finger stilled. "No, no, don't stop."

"Will you be my ol' lady, Taylor?"

"What?" His words didn't register because her brain was between her legs at the moment.

"Be my ol' lady, say yes, and I'll let you come."

He resumed his motions, but not with the rhythm required for her to orgasm.

His breath against her claiming mark and his slow fingers were torture.

"I'm already your mate, so—" Prowler cut her off before she could say the rest.

"It's not enough, Taylor." From his tone, he seemed to think she didn't understand how much it meant, but she did.

"I need to know you commit to all of me. Being with a King comes with certain risks and responsibilities, as does being with a shifter. The title of mate is important for one part of my life, but the title of ol' lady is important for the other."

Taylor knew what she was getting into with Prowler, not just the shifter world with its secrets, but the MC world too.

Being with someone who didn't always operate within the law came with inherent risks, ones that if you weren't ready for, would destroy you. But Taylor being Taylor, had made a list, and the Prowler column won every single time.

"Yes. I already consider myself your ol' lady. I was just waiting for you to catch up."

"Fuck." He thrust his hard cock between her

ass cheeks, sliding back and forth. When he angled his cock to dip between her legs, she turned and dropped to her knees.

Running her hands up his thighs, she tipped her head back in the direction of his face and licked her lips.

One of his hands threaded in her hair, holding her still. When he rubbed the head of his cock against her lips, her tongue darted out to chase it.

"There's my queen." His praise did things to her she never expected. Yeah, apparently, he'd unlocked a praise kink.

"If I'm your queen, then it's my job to show you that it's good to be king."

With that, she gripped his ass, bringing him to her mouth since she couldn't bring her mouth to him. When she swallowed as much of his cock as she could manage, he howled.

"Fuck yes, it's good to be king."

Want more motorcycle riding alphas?
Then check out, *Desert Phantoms MC.*

Start with book 1, Thunder...or if you're the type of reader who loves to read every mention, you can grab The Black Stetson, (Bullseye) the unofficial meet & greet with some of the members.

How do you feel about badass chicks kicking ass, riding motorcycles, & loving who and how they want?
If you love 'em as much as me, try my Shadow Angels MC.
Crossing Styx book 1
Styx is the SAMC enforcer with as much attitude as she has curves.
Check it out!

PLAYLIST
This is the playlist the characters in this book listen to.
I listened to it as well while writing the book to connect with them.

NO endorsement by the artists or their representatives is given or implied by sharing this list.
I hold no rights to any music/song listed here.

ACKNOWLEDGMENTS

Out of the gate, it's family. Always has been, always will be. They deserve so much more than a few lines, but that's all they're getting.

To the entire KOAMC family and its organizers. Thank you so much. I was completely humbled to be invited to be a part of this amazing world. Seriously, I am so not worthy, but you're stuck with me now, deal with it.

Ellie and Tina, as always thanks for having my back even when you know, without fail, I'm coming in hot and asking the impossible of you two, you deliver, and I can't thank you enough. Mine, an extra heap of love for the line work with promo.

Vixens, I love you, yet when I'm in the writing cave, I ignore you, but you still manage to always be there for me, and I can't put into words how amazing you are.

Shout out to Theresa Hissong for letting me use her book for Taylor's book shelf.

Backstage Bar & Billiards, you get a nod and a pretty big one. Every time I needed a mental metal break so I could actually write this damn book and not go insane, you delivered with some epically face-melting concerts. Thanks for that!

(Oh, and FYI, the "local band" they went to see in chapter 6, I didn't make them up, they're real. You should check 'em out.)

As always, if I left you off, insert your personal note here.

Yours in smut,
   Verlene \m/

BOOKS BY VERLENE

ANTHOLOGIES

Vegas Strong

AUDIO

Ryder Hard

ORDERED SERIES *(best read in order)*

Snagged by Hook *RBMC 2*

Infected by Virus *RBMC 3*

<u>SHADOW ANGELS MC</u>

Crossing Styx *SAMC 1*

ALTERNATING ORDERED SERIES *(multi-author series)*

<u>IRON TRAVELERS MC (Texas)</u>

Clear Your Mind *ITMC 1*

** Restore Your Faith *ITMC 2*

STAND-ALONE

Dangerous Curve Ahead

DIY Hearts

Exit the Friend Zone

Loving the Burn *(originally Control Line)*

Loving the Dream *(originally Unveiled)*

Loving the Ride *(originally Beckon)*

Ryder Hard

Second Chance Detour

The Black Stetson

The Black Stetson is the unofficial prequel to the DPMC series. It doesn't need to be read, but is the fun back story of Bullseye and the introduction of some of the brothers.

** By another author as part of the ordered series.

ABOUT VERLENE

Verlene was born and raised in the south, and pens smoking hot tales of life, lust, and love.

Thanks to the military, she's traveled the US but now calls Sin City home...again.

A self-proclaimed zombie apocalypse enthusiast, word porn peddler, human canvas, Manowarrior, serial grammar killer, rabid Bama fan, accidental dust bunny population specialist, and Harley riding, abuser of the word f*ck. A lover of all things Lemmy, wine, skulls, and metal.

She's thrown live grenades, survived the tear gas chamber, and forced road marches but still believes writing and self-publishing are more brutal.

Verlene's current published works include contemporary romance series, anthology contributions, sci-fi romance, and several stand-alone reads with various contemporary themes. Look for exciting new releases from her in paranormal, MFM, and who knows what else.

Verlene is on a mission to make naughty the new normal, one book at a time.

Find my book info, links, merch, signed books, ebooks, and all things Verlene here :
VerleneLandon.com

Sign up for my newsletter today. Not only will you get the latest Verlene news, subscribers' only giveaways, and exclusive content delivered to your inbox about once a month, you can download a free Verlene tale immediately.

SUBSCRIBE
https://bit.ly/3QsXbqm

KOAMC WORLD AUTHORS

Amy Davies

Andi Lynn

Andi Rhodes

Avelyn Paige

Barbara Nolan

Bink Cummings

Carmen Jenner

Chelle C. Craze

Chelsea Camaron

Christine Michelle

Ciara St. James

Claire C. Riley

Dani Rene

Darlene Tallman

D M Earl

E.C. Land

E. M. Shue

Glenna Maynard

Hilary Storm

India R Adams

Janine Infante Bosco

Jeanne St. James

Jessa Aarons

Jordan Marie

Jules Ford

Kathleen Kelly

KL Donn

Kristine Allen

Liberty Parker

M. Merin

Madalyn Judge

Madeline Sheehan

Manda Mellett

Max Henry

Michelle Dups

Morgan Jane Mitchell

Naomi Porter

Nikki Landis

Ryan Michele

Sapphire Knight

Verlene Landon

Winter Travers